BOOTS & THE ROGUE

UGLY STICK SALOON BOOK #13

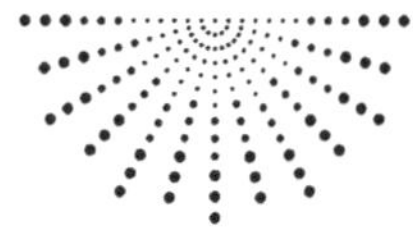

MYLA JACKSON

TWISTED PAGE INC

BOOTS & THE ROGUE

UGLY STICK SALOON SERIES BOOK #13

New York Times & USA Today
Bestselling Author

ELLE JAMES

writing as

MYLA JACKSON

Thanks to all my readers who keep coming back for more and making it possible for me to continue my writing career—I love you!

"Mom? Angus? I'm home!" Brody McFarlan pushed through the front door of the Rafter M Ranch main house. Stepping into the old colonial home was like stepping back into his childhood.

Nothing much had changed, other than a slightly different color of paint on the wall and maybe a new easy chair he hadn't noticed the last time he was there over a year ago.

"Mom?" he called out again, his heart bunching in his chest. Angus's and Colin's trucks weren't out front, and Brody hadn't driven around behind the house to see if his brothers had parked out by the barn. Damn. Had he arrived too late?

Pushing past the exhaustion of driving over twenty-five hours straight, he ran through the house, checking in his mother's bedroom and the kitchen. He was headed for the back door leading off the kitchen when it slammed open and a little boy of about five burst through, followed by a small golden retriever puppy with huge paws, yapping at his heels.

"You can't catch me!" the little boy shouted over his shoulder and barreled through the kitchen, slamming into Brody's legs.

The puppy sat back on his haunches in an attempt to stop, skidded across the wooden floor and bumped into the back of the little boy's knees, knocking him over.

Brody staggered backward, wondering if he'd wandered into the wrong house.

A female voice called from outside, "Dalton! Don't run in the house!" Seconds later, a gorgeous auburn-haired woman pushed through the door and stopped, her eyes rounded. "Oh, sorry. Can I help you?"

Brody stared at the boy and dog. "Do these belong to you?"

The woman laughed. "As a matter of fact, they do." She tilted her head and stared hard at him. "You look familiar."

"I'm sorry I can't say the same."

Her eyes rounded and she grinned. "You must be Brody." She leaned out the door. "Angus, sweetheart, come see who's here."

Heavy footsteps clunked against the wood planks of the deck outside and Brody's brother Angus filled the door behind the woman. He looped his arm around her waist and nuzzled her neck before he glanced up. "Who's here?"

When his gaze met Brody's he broke out in a huge smile. "Brody!"

The boy at Brody's feet stood and gathered the wiggling puppy in his arms. "Are you my Uncle Brody?"

"Well, actually—" the woman started but was cut off by more footsteps clomping against the deck.

"Angus! Gwen! Did you see which way Dalton and Shotgun went?" Brody's mother, Maggie McFarlan, burst through the door, her cheeks red, hair windblown and eyes sparkling. Far from the image Brody had in mind of a woman on the verge of death. "Oh, there he is. Thank goodness. I thought he might have gotten into the pen with the bull again." She glanced up and smiled. "Hello, Brody, it's good to see you." Then she blinked and the color drained from her face. "Brody?"

Brody nodded. "Hey, Mom."

Her eyes glistened with tears and she took a step toward him, then another and flung her arms around him, nearly tripping over the little boy at his feet. "Oh, Brody, I've missed you so much."

Brody hugged his mother long and hard. He had to swallow several times to loosen his constricted vocal cords. "I missed you too."

When he had a grip on his emotions, he held her at arm's length, scanning her face. "How are you? What does the doctor say? Why are you outside running around? Shouldn't you be in bed or in an easy chair resting?"

She frowned up at him and laughed. "What are you talking about? I'm fine."

More footsteps pounded across the deck outside the kitchen. "Hey, who left the door open on the chicken coop? There are chickens everywhere. I could use a hand getting them all back in the—" Colin, Brody's younger brother, banged through the door and came to a dead standstill.

Brody glared at him over his mother's head. "I drove twenty-five hours straight to get here."

"Oh, sweetheart." His mother cupped his cheek. "You must be exhausted."

"I am," he said through clenched teeth.

"Why didn't you take the usual three days?" she asked.

"Tell her." Brody's glare deepened.

Colin had the decency to blush. "Uh, could I get some help rounding up the chickens?"

Their mother frowned, her gaze shooting between Colin and Brody. "What's going on?"

Brody's anger simmered. "Colin called me exactly twenty-five hours ago to tell me you were sick, maybe dying. I dropped everything and came as fast as I could."

The little boy tugged on Brody's sleeve. "Are you my Uncle Brody?"

Brody looked down at the boy and back up to his mother and Angus. "Who are these people?"

Everyone talked at once until the cacophony of voices sounded like fans at a boxing match.

His head aching, his eyes burning from lack of sleep, Brody raised his hand and shouted, "Quiet!"

As if someone had turned the sound off on the radio, the kitchen got dead silent. Then the puppy in the boy's arms barked.

Angus took the dog from the boy and leaned in to hug Brody. "Hey, bro, glad you finally made it home. I'd like you to meet my girl, Gwen, and her boy, Dalton. The dog's name is Shotgun because he's fast out the barrel and scatters everywhere at once."

Gwen held out her hand. "Hello, Brody. Angus has told me so much about you. Well, about you as a boy growing up on the ranch. Nice to meet you."

Brody took her hand and shook it, his gaze going to Angus. "Your girl? Why didn't I know about this?"

"I'm sorry," his mother said. "It all happened so fast and I haven't talked to you in several weeks."

"You'd have known, if you'd been here," Colin said.

The silence stretched again.

"Well, now you are. Have a seat. Angus will make coffee, won't you, dear?" his mother said.

"What the h—" Brody glanced at the boy, and changed his expletive, "—heck is going on here?"

"Is Uncle Brody always mad?" Dalton asked, backing into Angus's legs, his eyes wide.

"No, Uncle Brody isn't always mad. Only for the last eight years," Colin said.

Angus shot him a killer look. "Mom, why don't you take Gwen and Dalton out and show them how to lead the chickens into the pen with a bucket of feed?"

"Oh boy!" Dalton ran for the door.

Mrs. McFarlan hooked Gwen's arm. "Come on, the boys need a little brotherly bonding time."

Colin snorted.

Their mother pointed at Colin and Brody. "Play nice and remember what I said." She shifted her gaze to include Angus and then stepped out the door.

Gwen shot a questioning glance at Angus and hustled Dalton out in front of her.

Once the women and the little boy were out of the house, Brody glared at his brothers. "What the hell is going on?"

"Sit." Angus pointed to the table.

Neither Colin nor Brody made a move to comply with his order.

Angus sighed. "Fine. Stand. But this might take a while to tell."

Colin broke in. "Mom's going to sell the ranch."

"What?" Brody looked from Colin back to Angus.

"Thanks, Colin." Angus shook his head. "Mom isn't selling the ranch; she's threatening to sell the ranch."

"Threatening?" Brody shook his head. "And you're sure she's not sick?"

"Cancer-free her last checkup. She's healthier than a horse."

Some of the tension Brody had carried with him from Seattle released. But this conversation was far from over. "Good. I'm glad she's doing better. But what did she mean by 'remember what I said'?"

Angus shoved a hand through his hair, standing it on end. "A couple weeks ago she told us that if the McFarlan men didn't show an interest in their inheritance, she was going to sell the Rafter M Ranch and everything on it."

"You and Colin have been here. I haven't. What's been going on to think you two aren't interested in the ranch?" Brody nodded toward Angus. "Aren't you raising horses and making a good go of it?"

Angus nodded. "Yeah, but that's not what she was talking about. She thinks there won't be any little McFarlans to pass the ranch down to."

"She wants us all married and having kids within two months. We're already down two weeks and have only six more to make it happen."

"What in the hell is he talking about?" Brody asked the oldest McFarlan brother.

"Just what Colin said—Mom wants us settled down, married or engaged by the end of the two months or she'll sell."

"Mrs. Reinhardt has been bragging about her grand-babies, and Mom is afraid she'll miss out unless she takes drastic measures," Colin inserted.

Angus nodded.

Brody stared at Angus. "Is that what Gwen and her boy are all about? Mom forced you into a relationship to save the ranch?"

"Yes...no...ah hell." Angus paced the length of the kitchen and back. "It started out that way."

Again, Colin jumped in with "Mom put my and Angus's name in the hat at the annual Ugly Stick Saloon bachelor auction. Gwen bought Angus for four dates and the rest is history."

Angus frowned at Colin. "Gwen and I knew each other seven years ago. I loved her then, but things didn't work out. The auction brought us back together." He smiled as he spoke. "I love Gwen and Dalton."

Brody was happy his brother had found a woman to share his life.

When Angus glanced up, his smile faded. "But we stand to lose the ranch if Mom's demands aren't met."

Brody crossed his arms. "And what does that have to do with me?"

"She wants all three of us married or on our way to being married within her two-month time frame. And she wants you home."

"Well, you got me home. But I'm not here to stay or to get married. I came because I thought Mom was sick." Again he threw another glare at Colin.

Colin pushed back his shoulders. "Would you have come if I'd asked?"

"Hell no."

"Would you have come if Angus had told you what was going on?" Colin continued.

Angus and Colin both stared at him, waiting for his answer.

"No," Brody said.

Colin's lips thinned and Angus's twisted in disappointment.

"This might not be home to you," Angus said, "but it's my home and I want to keep it."

"Mom is bluffing." Brody waved his hand at the kitchen with the copper-bottom pans his father had bought for their mother. She kept the copper polished and shiny. "She'd never sell the Rafter M. It has too many good memories of her life with Dad and us as kids growing up here. Hell, the place has been in our family for over a hundred years."

"One hundred fifty," Colin offered.

"I don't want to see it split up and sold, any more

than Colin does," Angus said. "I'm not sure what your job situation is—"

Brody held up his hand. "Don't even go there. I'm not staying."

Angus went on, "And I'm not asking you to stay forever, just stay long enough to get Mom to retract her ultimatum."

"I have a life in Seattle," he lied. He lived in Seattle, but he didn't know many more people in the big city than when he'd landed there eight years ago and found a temporary job as a bartender that he still worked part time while he pursued his second job, his real passion. "I can't hang around here until Mom changes her mind."

"At least stay until the end of the two months. Give Mom that. She loves you and wants to see you more often."

"She can come to Seattle. The road goes both ways."

"She wants you to come home," Angus insisted.

"What he means is Mom wants the two of us to kiss and make up," Colin finished.

Brody narrowed his eyes and stared at his younger brother. Because of Colin, he'd left home in the first place. Because his own brother betrayed him with the woman he was about to marry. He shook his head. "Not happening."

"Eight years is a long time to hold a grudge," Colin said. "I told you then I was sorry. What happened between me and Fancy shouldn't have, and I've regretted it ever since."

"You're damn right it shouldn't have happened."

Brody crossed to stand in front of Colin. "Who can you trust if you can't trust your own brother?"

Angus stared at Colin, a frown drawing his brows together. "You slept with Brody's fiancé?"

Colin's gaze never waivered from Brody's. "We didn't mean for it to happen. She was upset…one thing led to another…" He shook his head. "We shouldn't have done it, and we haven't seen each other since."

A long silence stretched between the brothers.

"Eight years, Brody," Angus finally said. "That's a long time. We're family."

Brody snorted. "That's what I thought, until my brother betrayed me."

Colin shook his head. "I told you it wouldn't do any good."

"Colin…" Angus pinned the youngest McFarlan with the same stern stare their father used on them when they were in trouble as children, "…would you go help the women."

Colin stood still for a moment longer, and then he turned and left the kitchen without another word.

"Whatever you have to say, I'm not listening. As soon as I've had a decent dinner and ten hours' sleep, I'm on the road back to Seattle."

Angus crossed the room and stood in front of Brody. "Fair enough." Then he hugged Brody hard. "I've missed you, brother."

When he stood back, the moisture in Angus's eyes could not be mistaken. That alone tugged hard at Brody's heart. "Two weeks. I'll stay for two weeks."

Angus nodded. "Thanks. Hopefully, within two

weeks we can talk Mom out of selling the ranch, and we can all get back to living our lives, drama-free."

That settled, Brody's stomach grumbled. "What I've missed is Mom's fried chicken. Do you think she'll cook that for dinner?"

Angus grimaced. "Oh, one other thing. As part of Mom's move-on-or-move-out ultimatum, she's on strike. She's not cooking, cleaning or buying groceries. We're on our own for food and laundry."

"You're kidding, right?"

"I wish I were." His face brightened. "I don't suppose you've picked up some cooking skills in your eight years on the West Coast?"

"I eat out all the time. I even burn toast." His stomach growled. "What do you do for dinner around here?"

"We eat at the diner in Temptation for the most part, but the Ugly Stick Saloon is having a barbeque tonight on account of the rodeo being in town. Gwen and Dalton are headed back to Dallas this afternoon. Mom's having dinner at Mrs. Reinhardt's. Colin and I were headed to the Ugly Stick. You're welcome to join us."

"I'm beat after being on the road."

"Man, there is nothing in the refrigerator."

His stomach grumbled again, making the decision for him. "The Ugly Stick Saloon it is."

"You're gonna love what the new owner has done to the place."

"Yeah?"

"She's a retired stripper married to Jackson Gray Wolf. They're about to have their first kid."

Brody's chest tightened. So much had changed at home. The Ugly Stick was under new ownership. His friend Jackson Gray Wolf had succumbed to the institution of marriage and his mother had gone off her rocker with crazy threats. He should have stayed in Seattle and forgotten Temptation, Texas, ever existed.

CHAPTER TWO

Jessie Taylor reined in her horse at the only building she'd passed in the last five miles. The sign over the top of the tin structure tilted to one side, but had big, western-style lettering proclaiming it as the Ugly Stick Saloon.

Hot, tired, homeless and having left her car behind to save her horse, she wondered what else could go wrong this dramatic day. Too dispirited to think that far ahead, she melted out of the saddle and almost collapsed on wobbly legs. Yeah, she rode horses often, but rarely for thirty miles in a single day.

She clung to the saddle until her legs remembered what it was like to walk. Then she pushed her hat back on her head and scanned the outside of the building, hoping to find a water hose somewhere.

She needed to cool down and Scout needed at least a gallon of water to drink before he passed out from dehydration. Why of all days did Imelda Funk have to show up at the boarding stable where Jessie worked, to find her husband Billy Ray hitting on Jessie? The woman never came to the stable, whereas Jessie had been fending off Billy Ray's overtures for months, each time telling the pig-faced used-car dealer she was not, nor ever would be, interested in rolling in the hay with him.

Unfortunately, her boss had witnessed the whole showdown between Jessie, Billy Ray and Imelda. He'd fired her on the spot and would have turned Scout loose when she didn't have enough money to pay his boarding, part of her former compensation package, which was nothing more than indentured servitude.

Silas Butts had taken advantage of her when she'd been desperate to find a place she could keep her horse and work for enough to put a meager roof over her head. He'd even offered to let her live in the stable's office, which happened to have a shower and a hot plate, everything she needed to live.

In return for his generosity, she worked the entire boarding stable, looking after the thirty horses that had to be fed, groomed and cleaned up after.

When he fired her, he turned her and Scout out in the road.

Jessie had to make a choice between her car and her horse. Since Scout was the horse her father had given her before he died, she couldn't just turn him loose and hope a truck didn't hit him. She'd packed as much of her meager belongings as she could into a backpack, rolled the quilt that had belonged to her grandmother into a plastic bag, saddled Scout and rode away, leaving her car behind. If Silas didn't have it hauled off, she'd have to come back another day to claim it. Preferably when she had enough money to put gas in the tank.

About as down-and-out as a person could get, she wanted to cry, but she was too hot and dry to shed a single tear, and her horse needed water before she could collapse into a pitiful heap.

Leading Scout around to the back of the building, she spotted a spigot near the back door and hurried toward it, her mouth like cotton and her face hot and sweaty from riding for the past eight hours. As she bent to turn on the water, the back door opened and a strawberry-blonde-haired woman backed out of the door, dragging a large trash bag. As soon as the woman cleared the door, she straightened and pressed a hand to the small of her back, her belly protruding like she'd swallowed a basketball.

"Holy smokes," Jessie said out loud, then clamped a hand over her mouth.

"What the—?" The woman spun and teetered on the edge of the concrete porch.

Jessie rushed forward and steadied her before she fell and busted open like a ripe watermelon falling off the back of a farm truck.

"Oh dear, thank you," the woman said, getting her balance and stepping down from the porch.

"Ma'am, should you be carrying something so heavy when you're so…so…" Jessie fought for a polite way of saying it.

"Ginormous? Is that the word you were looking for?"

Jessie backed away, her eyes wide. "No, ma'am. I wouldn't say that. Why you're the prettiest thing I've seen, even as…as… Ah hell, I'll be going before I put my other foot in my mouth."

"No, don't." The woman rubbed her hands down the side of her maternity jeans and then held one out. "I'm Audrey Anderson, owner of the Ugly Stick Saloon." She laughed. "I know. I don't look much like the owner of a saloon."

Jessie took her hand and the woman gave her a firm shake. She liked her already. "Jessie Taylor. Owner of practically nothing but this horse and the clothes on my back." She nodded toward the spigot. "I hope you don't mind, but Scout and I could use a drink of water before we move on."

"Oh, sweetie, by all means, drink as much as you want, only wouldn't you rather have a bucket for the horse and a cup for yourself?"

Jessie shrugged. "Scout and I don't mind drinking out of the spigot. We're used to it."

"Tell you what…" Audrey smiled, "…I'll pay you twenty dollars to put this bag into that bin over there, while I find a clean bucket for your horse. And then you're coming inside for a glass of ice water."

"I'll carry the bag for you." Jessie pushed her tired shoulders back. "But you don't have to pay me to do it. I don't need charity."

"I'm not offering charity. I'm offering to pay you for work performed." Audrey cocked her brows. "So are you going to help a poor pregnant lady out and work for her, or do I have to carry this big bag of trash to that bin way over there?"

Jessie tied Scout's reins to the porch rail and easily lifted the bag onto her shoulder. It took all of five seconds to do the work and Jessie returned to an empty porch.

A minute later, Audrey carried an empty mop bucket out and handed it to Jessie. "You'll need to rinse it before you let your horse drink out of it, but it'll do for now."

Audrey stood in the doorway, fanning herself with the cool air from inside of the saloon, while she waited for Jessie to water her horse.

With an audience, Jessie hurried, splashing water on her jeans as she sloshed water in the bucket and cleaned it thoroughly before filling it full of fresh, cool liquid.

Scout nudged her back and whinnied, eager for a drink.

Jessie set the bucket on the ground in front of her horse and patted his hot neck. "I'm sorry," she whispered, staring down at the crystal-clear water, her mouth as dry as the Texas summer.

"Come on, I've got a tall, cool glass of water with your name on it inside." Audrey held the door wide and waited for Jessie to climb the porch steps and enter the darkened interior of the saloon.

Thankfully, Audrey took the lead.

After being outside all day in the brilliant sunshine, it took a minute for Jessie's vision to adjust to the dim lighting. They walked down a long hallway with doors on either side and emerged into the saloon behind the bar.

"Sit," Audrey commanded, pointing to the barstools on the other side of the counter.

"If you don't mind, I'd prefer to stand. I've been in the saddle all day."

"Whatever melts your butter, sweetie." Audrey scooped ice into a large beer mug and filled it with water. She set it in front of Jessie and filled another the same way. Then she came out from behind the counter and sat on the stool Jessie had declined. "So, what's your story?"

Jessie took a moment to down the full glass of icy-cold water before answering, "I don't have much of a story."

"Help yourself to the water or anything else you might like to drink." Audrey nodded toward the bar and took a sip of her own water. "I find that everyone has a story, but not everyone likes to tell it until they get to know who they're telling it to." Audrey laughed at her own words.

The woman had such a cheerful demeanor Jessie couldn't help but feel better in her presence. Until her thoughts returned to the fact she was homeless, jobless and didn't have a place to stable Scout. She shrugged, not wanting to burden this nice woman with her own problems, when she appeared to be ready to deliver her baby at any moment.

For a terrifying second, Jessie considered what would happen if Audrey did deliver while she was there, apparently the only one in the saloon with the owner.

Audrey slid a hand over her baby bump and sighed. "It's the calm before the storm here. Everyone is at the rodeo. In the next fifteen minutes I expect my staff to come through the doorway."

"I'll be sure to get out of your way well before then, ma'am." Jessie rounded the back of the bar and filled her mug again.

"I expect with the rodeo crowd here, I'll be swamped and shorthanded as usual and we're having a barbeque to boot." She glanced up at Jessie, her eyes narrowing, calculating. "I don't suppose you know how to grill burgers and hot dogs, do you?"

"Yes, ma'am. I used to grill for the ranch hands when my father was the foreman of the Circle C Ranch. During branding season, we'd have fifteen or twenty mouths to feed. I was in charge of the grill. Why?"

"If you would stick around for the night, I could sure use the help. It would save me from trying to stand for hours with this bowling ball in front of me."

Jessie stared at the woman. "You weren't going to do all the grilling like…that, were you?"

Audrey shrugged. "I still haven't quite realized my limitations. But, today, I'm feeling it." She pressed her hand to her back again. "I had my brother-in-law lined up to do it, but he and my husband have a horse down and will be staying with her until she's out of danger."

Jessie nodded. "Understandable. I'm actually better with horses than cooking. Perhaps I could go sit with the horse while your brother-in-law does the grilling."

"Oh no." Audrey shook her head. "Mark wouldn't leave a horse while she's down, and I wouldn't ask him to. I told him I'd have one of the waitresses fill in for him. I have a feeling we'll be too busy to pull a waitress out of the saloon to cook, so I was going to man the grill."

"I'd be happy to take over the grill. But you don't have to pay me. I'd do it for the price of a hamburger." Jessie's belly rumbled at the thought of a juicy grilled burger.

"I wouldn't hear of it. If you grill for me, you're on the payroll and one of the perks is free food. That is, if you're up to it."

Jessie stared down at her dusty jeans. As tired as she was from riding all day, she wouldn't turn down a job if it meant enough cash to buy a meal or two until she could find a job and a place to stay. She'd been aiming for Temptation, the small Texas town in the middle of nowhere. The farther away from Shady Creek Horse Boarding and the Dallas horse owners who frequented it, the better. "I'm up to it. But I really need to shower and put on some clean clothes."

"We have a bathroom with a shower in the backstage area of the saloon." Audrey grinned. "We like our cowboys oiled up for Ladies' Night at the Ugly Stick. And they don't like to get into their trucks until they've had a chance to rinse off."

Jessie's brows rose with the heat in her cheeks. What kind of place was this?

Audrey laughed. "Relax. We only have Ladies' Night once a month when we bring in male strippers. Gives the ladies a little release. Our strippers are homegrown, and it gives them a lot of extra spending money. A win-win situation."

"Oh. Okay." Jessie set her mug in the sink behind the bar and jerked her thumb over her shoulder. "I'll just get my clean jeans."

Audrey stood. "If it's all the same to you, we have tons of costumes backstage. In honor of the rodeo and the cowboys who live the rough life, the ladies who work at the Ugly Stick Saloon dress up as our favorite vintage heroines. Women like Calamity Jane, the Madam Mollie Johnson—Queen of the Deadwood Blondes—and Annie Oakley. Last year I came as the pistol-packing, notorious outlaw Belle Starr. This year, I'll be the Unsinkable Molly Brown, complete with my own buoy." She patted her belly. "Come on, I'll show you what we have."

Jessie hung back. "I don't know. I'm not much of a girlie girl."

"Then you can be Annie Oakley. She wasn't either. Though she wore a dress, she was one of the best shots in the Old West. She traveled with Buffalo Bill's Wild West show."

"I know who Annie Oakley was." Though Jessie had never been to college, she read everything she could get her hands on, including biographies in the school library. She'd had a great respect for the young sharpshooter and her rise to fame during a time when women were expected to stay home and raise babies. "I suppose I could dress as Annie Oakley."

"Good!"

Audrey showed Jessie to the room behind the stage

and the many racks of costumes, including chaps, whips, vests and hats.

"You can use that brush to dust off your cowboy boots and there's polish in that drawer if you want to put some color back into them. Nothing like a comfortable pair of boots to see you through the day." Audrey stared down at her belly. "Wish I could see my red boots." She sighed. "Not much longer and this baby and I will both be able to see my boots."

"If you don't mind me asking, when are you due?"

"No worries. Not for another sixteen weeks."

"Sixteen weeks?" Jessie's gaze slipped to Audrey's baby bump. "Shouldn't you be resting?"

"Exactly what I'll be doing, now that I have filled the position of grill master. The bathroom is in the corner and here's the Annie Oakley costume." She pulled out a tanned leather vest that was closer to a corset than anything.

The low-cut V neck had been trimmed in short leather fringe, with bright beads sewn in a pattern across the breast. The tanned leather skirt would barely come down to Jessie's knees, exposing her legs all the way down to the tops of her boots.

She glanced up at Audrey. "I don't remember Annie Oakley wearing a dress like that. Where's the rest of it?"

Audrey's laughter warmed her, at the same time that it worried her. "Oh, sweetie, you've never been to the Ugly Stick Saloon. The people who come to drink and party here like to see a little more skin than at a church picnic. Go on, get that shower and get dressed. The crowd will be arriving within an hour and we have to have at least a hundred burgers and dogs ready."

Jessie entered the bathroom and locked the door behind her, wondering if she could stay hidden there all night and nobody would notice. Her stomach grumbled, reminding her she hadn't had anything to eat in twenty-four hours. She would do practically anything for one night, as long as food was included.

THE PARKING LOT of the Ugly Stick Saloon was over-flowing by the time the McFarlan brothers arrived.

"Damn. I hope there isn't a line for the food," Brody said. "I could eat a side of beef all by myself, as hungry as I am."

"Knowing Audrey, she's had the grill fired up for a couple of hours already." Angus parked in a field and looked out at a brindle quarter horse tethered to the fence, chomping on the grass within reach. "Can't believe a cowboy would ride his horse all the way over from the arena."

"Maybe he has big plans to drink and doesn't want to get a DUI." Brody glanced at the horse. "That's one ugly horse."

"What are you talking about?" Angus frowned. "He's got great lines."

"I agree with Brody," Colin commented. "I never was a fan of that brindle coloring. Looks like someone splashed paint all over him."

Brody wondered if Colin was agreeing with him just because he was trying to suck up and make things right between the two of them. He ignored his younger brother, not ready to forgive him. Granted, he'd stopped thinking about Fancy less than a year after he left the Rafter M Ranch. But he hadn't stopped thinking about Colin screwing around with her the night after he asked her to marry him. Colin had known she said yes, had been there when he showed the ring to his family and announced his intentions.

His belly aching from more than hunger, Brody headed off across the field, making a beeline for the smoke rising higher than the saloon's rooftop. He could smell burgers charring and didn't want to dwell on the past until he'd filled his stomach.

Tables had been set up outside. Pretty waitresses dressed in corsets, frilly skirts and cowboy boots weaved between the guests, serving up plates of hamburgers, whiskey shooters and mugs of beer.

Several cowboys rose from the corner of the table nearest the grill and ambled into the saloon for music, dancing and more alcohol.

Brody claimed the spot and glanced around for the waitress. The closest one was occupied with a full table of dusty, sweaty and rowdy cowboys having come straight from riding rodeo events. They were loud and demanding. Brody didn't expect the waitress to make it over to him within the next fifteen minutes.

As close as he was to the grill, he could stand up and ask to be served next. The cook was a tall woman, maybe five eight or nine, with long sandy-blonde hair pulled back into a ponytail. She wore a short doeskin-leather dress that hugged her middle like a corset. On her feet were well-worn, but polished, cowboy boots. She flipped burgers, tossed on new ones and turned the hot dogs—all with quick, practiced flicks of her wrists. Every time she moved, the hem of the skirt swayed, emphasizing her tiny waist and the sexy flare of her hips, and exposing more of her toned thighs.

Brody frowned, fully hoping that when she turned she'd be fifty with an inch of makeup to hide the wrinkles, her eyes ringed in eyeliner so thick she'd look like a raccoon on his last legs. Unfortunately, her legs looked young and supple, like they'd easily wrap around a man's waist and hold on tight as he rode her to an incredible orgasm.

Hell, Brody wasn't there to ride a cowgirl or get involved in anything other than a hamburger loaded with pickles, onions and catsup. No, he'd had his share of the women of Temptation, Texas. If they were all like Fancy, he didn't need them.

Angus, Colin and another cowboy joined him at the table.

"Brody, good to see you." The cowboy reached across the table.

"You remember Jake Maddox, don't you?" Angus introduced the cowboy.

Brody's eyes narrowed. "Jake. The only Jake I remember was the one who could outrun me in track and was the smallest, but fastest, receiver we'd ever had on the football team." He gripped the man's hand and grinned. "Good to see you finally grew up. How tall are you?"

Jake chuckled. "Last I checked, I was six foot four."

"Damn, what did they feed you after high school?"

"Burgers and beer."

"Speaking of burgers…" Brody stood, "…I can't wait another minute." He rounded the table and headed for the cook.

Apparently, he wasn't the only one getting impatient with waiting for food. A huge, burly cowboy with a unibrow slashed across his forehead clomped between the tables and stopped beside the cook. "How's about giving me one of those burgers?" he said, his voice, like his body, big and rough.

The woman turned enough that Brody could see her face. Young, girl next door, no makeup and the leather vest was cut in a low V, exposing more of her chest than it covered, the gentle swells of her breasts filmed with a light coat of perspiration only adding to her overall appeal.

"Please take a seat, sir. The waitress will get your order," she said, her voice firm, her lips a soft pink and what Brody would consider highly kissable.

"I'm not sitting until I get my burger." He stepped closer. "I might even have me a little taste of the cook while I'm at it."

Brody took a step forward, putting himself between the cook and the burly cowboy. "The lady said 'take a seat'."

The cowboy raised ham-hock-sized fists. "You gonna make me?"

"No," Angus said from behind Brody. "But we will."

With a rustle of jeans and boots scuffing the ground, Angus, Colin and Jake rose from the table.

A waitress hurried over and hooked the big man's arm. "Hey, cowboy, have a seat so that I can get your order. It will only take a minute."

His eyes narrow, fists still clenched, the big man finally conceded. "S'long as I get my burger."

"You'll get it. Just no fighting." The woman led him back to his table and took his order.

"Thank you." The cook held out her hand. "I wasn't sure I could take him."

Brody chuckled when her grip tightened in his, strong and sure. "I'm betting you could."

"Jessie Taylor."

"Brody McFarlan." Brody sniffed the heaven of grilled burgers. "Do you work here at the Ugly Stick Saloon?"

"Only for tonight."

"Damn, those smell good."

She shrugged. "I try."

"Look, if you don't have other work lined up, I have a proposition for you."

Her brows dove into a V. "You jerk."

Before Brody could guess what would happen next, she plowed a fist into his eye and he went down, the late afternoon sunshine fading into black.

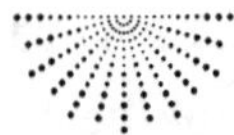

CHAPTER THREE

"Brody."

A voice called out to him, dragging him from the darkness back to the light.

"Brody!"

He blinked his eyes and winced as he stared up at Angus leaning over him, his brows knit.

"Hey, you okay?" his older brother asked.

"What happened?" Brody turned his head, noting the other faces gathered around in a circle over him. Then the image of a pretty fist powering into his face replayed in his head and he pressed a hand to his aching eye. "She hit me," he said.

"And I'd hit him again." The cook held the spatula like a weapon. "The bastard propositioned me!"

"What's going on?" A very pregnant woman waddled up to the crowd gathered around Brody.

"The chick decked him." The big brute who'd backed

down earlier busted out laughing, slapping a hand to his leg. "What a man."

Brody sat up, pressing his hand to his sore eye. "Who are you?"

"I'm Audrey, the owner of the Ugly Stick Saloon. And you are?"

Brody shoved a hand through his hair. "Brody McFarlan."

"One of the McFarlans, huh?" Audrey slipped an arm around the woman who'd hit him. "Are you all right, Jessie?"

"I'm fine, but that man came on to me, so I slugged him."

Audrey stared down at Brody. "Is that true? Did you make a pass at Jessie?"

"Hell no. I told her I had a proposition for her. I wanted to hire her on as a cook for the Rafter M Ranch." He pushed to his feet and swayed. "Damn, I guess I'm hungrier than I thought."

Jessie's eyes rounded and her mouth made an O. "I thought you were propositioning me."

Audrey shook her head. "Oh, Jessie, sweetie, we don't slug our customers. Serve Mr. McFarlan a burger, please. That's a good girl."

Brody settled on the bench.

Audrey snatched a chilled beer off the tray one of the waitresses carried and handed it to Brody. "Press that to your eye while I get some ice."

Feeling like a pansy-ass wuss having been floored by a girl, Brody swallowed half the beer and then pressed the chilled bottle to his throbbing eye.

Audrey waved her arms. "Show's over; get back to eating and drinking. Then when you're ready for a real show, come on inside the saloon. Hell for Leather is playing and the girls will be dancing."

As one, the men whooped and hollered, going back to their seats to finish off their beers and burgers.

Angus, Colin and Jake settled onto the benches around Brody.

"I'm thinking the diner might have been a better choice. How long has Mom been on strike?"

"Two weeks," Colin and Angus said at once.

"Damn. I can't cook."

"I've tried, but I burned water," Colin said.

Angus hung his head, staring at his hands. "The one time I cooked, we all ended up with food poisoning."

"Yeah and it didn't taste good going down or coming up." Colin leaned forward. "So what did you say to Jessie, the cook?"

"I told her I had a proposition for her." Brody winced as he pressed the bottle to his eye. "Apparently grilling for the Ugly Stick is a one-night deal and she doesn't have any other job to go to. The burgers smell good. No one seems to be dying from them. I thought she could take on the job of cook for the ranch. At least while I'm in town. I don't plan on starving or eating out every night."

Colin nodded, his face splitting into a grin. "Damned good idea."

"It was. Until she punched me in the face."

"A simple misunderstanding." Angus glanced over Brody's shoulder. "Shh. Here she comes with a burger."

The cook stopped next to Brody and slid a plate loaded with a burger and all the fixings under his nose. "Mr. McFarlan, I'm sorry I knocked you out. I thought you were coming on to me and...well...I misunderstood."

"Jessie, is it?" Colin started.

Brody held up his hand. "Colin," he warned.

His younger brother looked all innocent. "What? It was your idea in the first place."

"And a bad one."

"Not at all." Angus smiled at Jessie. "Jessie, I'm Angus McFarlan. These are my brothers, Colin and Brody. We need...no...the Rafter M Ranch needs a cook. If you want the job, you can have it."

Jessie chewed on her bottom lip. "I don't know."

"See? She doesn't want the job," Brody said.

"Oh, I want the job, but wherever I go to work I'll need room and board, and a place for my horse."

Brody glanced at the woman, his eyes narrowing. "Your horse?"

She tilted her chin up. "Yes, my horse. We're kind of a package deal."

"We have an extra bedroom in the house," Angus offered.

Jessie's brows pulled together. "One woman among three big men?" She shook her head.

"Three men and their mother. It's actually her house and her ranch."

"And your mother doesn't cook?" Jessie asked.

"Long story," Brody said.

Colin added, "The best part is that we have a few

thousand acres. I'm sure we can find room for one horse."

Brody fixed his stare on Jessie. "Your horse wouldn't be the ugly brindle tied to the fence out back?"

She drew herself up to her full height, which was taller than most women, and said, "Scout isn't ugly. He has character, and he's mine."

"Guys, we don't know anything about her," Brody argued.

"You were the one who first tried to proposition me," Jessie shot back. "Why the change of heart? Just because I could put you down with one punch?"

"Hell no." Brody realized that was exactly the reason. She'd embarrassed him in front of all those cowboys and his brothers. How could he live that down? Then again, it *had* been because of a misunderstanding and his own poor choice of words. "Okay, okay, if you want the job, you can have it."

"And Scout?"

Brody snorted, aware of the irony. "Yes, you and the horse you rode in on."

Jessie flung her arms around his neck. Her breasts, in that ridiculous shirt with the fringe, pressed firmly against his chest, made Brody's groin tighten and his throbbing eye twitch.

Colin pointed to the grill. "Your burgers are on fire."

Jessie squealed and spun toward the grill, quick to put the lid down to smother the flames.

Brody shook his head. What had he just committed to?

Angus pounded his back, grinning. "Don't worry,

brother. At least we'll have decent cooking. After we have that burger, Colin and I will head back to the ranch to grab a trailer for her horse."

"Damned ugly horse," Brody muttered. "Why am I not going with you?"

"You need to stay and make sure she doesn't get away." Angus's lips twisted into a wry grin. "We need her."

AN HOUR LATER, the last burger was cooked. Jessie cleaned the grill and headed into the saloon as the sun gave a brilliant performance in its descent across the western horizon.

The cowboys had either gone back to take care of their horses for the next day's rodeo events or gone inside to listen to the music and drink more beer.

Eager to help out any way she could, Jessie collected trash and dumped it in the bin behind the saloon. She took a brief moment to check on Scout, who had mowed all the grass in a half circle around the post he was tied to.

Jessie untied Scout and moved him and his water bucket to another post with more grass. "Don't you worry, we're going to have a new home with lots of hay and water and no Silas skimping on your feed."

She patted her horse and turned.

Brody McFarlan stood several feet away, leaning against a fence post, his cowboy hat pulled down low over his eyes. The sunset behind him outlined his broad shoulders and trim waist.

He had been the one to bring up the offer to hire her, but after she'd punched him, he hadn't seemed keen on having her come to work as the ranch cook. If she wanted it to work out, Jessie had to make things right between them.

"Mr. McFarlan, I'm sorry about the misunderstanding. I guess I was punchy after that big man, and, well, I've been in bad situations before."

She crossed to him, tipped his hat back and winced. The eye had swollen almost shut and started turning a deep shade of purple. "I did that?"

He nodded. "Yup."

"Your brothers kind of pushed you into following through with the offer to hire me. If you've changed your mind, I could just leave and you'll never have to see me again."

He shook his head before she'd finished her speech. "Can't. My brothers went back to the ranch for the horse trailer. I was given strict instructions to keep an eye on you so you don't get away."

She frowned. "Are you sure you have a mother out at that ranch of yours? I mean, you aren't going to take me out in the middle of nowhere and force me into slave labor or the sex trade, are you?" She chewed on her bottom lip. "You know, this is a bad idea. I don't know you or your ranch."

He pulled his cell phone from his pocket. "I can call our mother and have her vouch for us, if you like."

"Yes, please."

He hit the number for home and waited. When his

mother answered, he said, "Mom, have Angus and Colin made it home yet?"

He listened.

Jessie could hear a female voice talking.

"They didn't tell you?" he said. "We're hiring a cook and they're bringing the trailer for the horse… No, the cook isn't a horse. Here, say hello to Jessie and tell her it isn't just men out at the ranch." Brody handed the phone to Jessie.

She held it to her ear. "Hi, this is Jessie."

"Jessie, so very nice to meet you. Well, to meet your voice, anyway. I'm glad the boys finally decided to hire a cook. I thought for a while there they'd be too stubborn and end up starving to death. But don't you worry. I have a nice room for you next to mine, and if any one of my boys does something stupid, they're not too big to turn over my knee."

Jessie laughed, her gaze going to the cowboy leaning against the fence post. He had to be at least six two or three. The idea of his mother turning him over her knee was ridiculous. "Thank you, Mrs. McFarlan. I look forward to meeting you in person."

She ended the call and handed the phone back to Brody. When their hands touched in the exchange, an electric shock zipped through her fingers and up her arm, making her tingle all over. She jerked her hand back and rubbed her arm.

"Feel better?" he asked.

Yes and no. Yes, that there was a mother at the ranch and, no, because of the shock she'd experienced touching the man. "A little. I'd better get back inside and see if there is anything else I can do for Audrey."

"You'll have to go around front. The back door locks automatically when it closes."

"Oh, okay." She hurried around the side of the building, annoyed that Brody kept pace with her, opening the door to the saloon for her.

Jessie wasn't used to people opening doors for her. She'd been around cowboys all her life and then worked at a stable where she was the one to open doors for the clients who boarded their horses there. It felt strange and yet she found she liked it.

Audrey waddled by. "Oh, Jessie, I'm glad you're done outside. Could I get you to restock the coolers behind the bar? Libby, the bartender, will tell you what to get out of the storeroom. Jackson won't let me lift anything heavier than my purse." She leaned close. "He has spies watching me." She winked and hurried to help a waitress distribute drinks at one of the larger tables.

Jessie headed toward the bar, figuring one of the doors along the hallway behind the bar had to be the storeroom. As she reached the hall, a large woman built like a football linebacker stepped in front of her. "Employees only beyond this point."

Not knowing who this woman was or where else to go for the alcohol, Jessie turned toward the bar.

A pretty woman with auburn hair, flashing green eyes and a towel thrown over her shoulder saved Jessie from guessing. "Hi, I'm Libby Jones, the bartender. You must be Jessie. Audrey said you'd be helping out as soon as we ran out of burgers outside." She turned to the large woman. "Jessie, this is Greta Sue, our bouncer. Greta Sue, Jessie is an employee of the Ugly Stick Saloon for tonight. I need her to help restock the coolers."

Greta glanced over Jessie's shoulder. "What about him?"

Jessie and Libby turned as one.

Brody stood with his arms crossed. "I'm the muscle. If any really heavy items need lifting, I'm your man."

Jessie bristled. "I can handle anything."

"I can help too," Greta Sue offered. As soon as the words left the woman's mouth, a fight broke out between two cowboys on the other side of the saloon. "On second thought, I better go break up some of their fun." Greta Sue pushed through the crowd bent on joining the ruckus.

"Sweetie…" Libby touched Jessie's arm, "…let your man help. I'm down four cases of beer and two cases of whiskey. First door on the left is the storeroom." She gave them the brand names of the alcohol she needed and raced back to the bar where a line of thirsty cowboys had formed.

"I can handle this myself," Jessie insisted. Her father didn't raise a weak female. And the work she'd done at the boarding stables had been arduous, building her muscles and keeping her lean and fit.

"You heard the bartender. She needs her hard liquor and beer restocked ASAP." Brody pushed past Jessie and entered the first door on the left.

Jessie snorted. "Arrogant male."

Brody poked his head out of the door. "I heard that.

Remember, my brothers will kill me if I let you out of my sight."

"I'm not going anywhere. Tonight, I work for Audrey. I've already agreed to come to work at the Rafter M. I can start tomorrow."

"And how will you get from here to there?"

She lifted her chin. "I have Scout."

"And we want breakfast bright and early. If I leave you to find your own way to the ranch, you might get lost." He shook his head. "You're stuck with me. So shut up and put up. There's a saloon full of thirsty cowboys out there; you don't want Libby to run out of booze. Such a travesty could cause a riot." Brody's dark eye glistened with humor. The swollen one caused her to rethink her stubborn refusal of help.

Jessie pressed her lips together. "Okay. You can get the whiskey cases. I'll carry the beer."

They took turns carrying boxes through the door and unloading them behind the bar, meeting back in the storeroom for the next cases and the next.

"I could use the Patrón next," Libby said on their last pass. "It's on one of the top shelves in the back. You might have to look for it. No hurry. I still have half a bottle left."

Back in the storeroom, Jessie pulled a step stool up to the back row of shelves and climbed to the top.

"Do you want me to get it down?" Brody asked, standing at the bottom of the stool, his hands on either side of her.

Butterflies fluttered in her belly and warmth built deep inside, spreading outward. Jessie's cheeks flushed and she had a hard time focusing on the boxes in front of her. The man affected her more than she cared to admit and having him hover beneath her was driving her crazy.

Focus.

She located the case of Patrón and pulled one bottle out of the box, handing it down to Brody.

He took the bottle and set it aside. "Now come down before you fall off that ladder."

"I'm going to grab one more bottle." Jessie pulled the bottle out of the box and bent to hand it down to Brody. With him looking up at her, she lost her focus again and, with it, her balance.

"Oh no." She flailed with her empty hand, searching for something to grab hold of to steady her. Her hand only met air and she fell, clutching to her chest the bottle of expensive tequila. Strong arms reached out to catch her, breaking her fall.

Jessie crashed against Brody's chest and sent him staggering a couple steps backward before he steadied himself, holding her close.

With her heart pounding like a manic bass drum, she sucked in a deep breath and stared up at the cowboy who'd saved her twice that day. Her face was so close to his, she could lean forward a little bit and their lips would touch.

Brody's jaw was set, strong and peppered with a dark beard shadow, and his lips were full and...and... downright kissable. She trembled with the effort to resist his mouth. She'd never been that tempted by a man. Although she'd lost her virginity as a teen, she had little experience with men, other than a bit of kissing, groping in the dark and finally sex that left her feeling like there ought to be more.

Brody, on the other hand, seemed like he'd be the "more" she'd been expecting those other times she'd gotten intimate with men.

She glanced up, her heart fluttering when she realized he'd been staring at her mouth as well.

Jessie swept her tongue across her bottom lip.

"You really should be more careful," he said.

His arms tightened and he crushed her to him, his mouth claiming hers in a kiss that rocked her to her core.

Jessie's lips parted on a gasp and he took advantage, his tongue sweeping past her teeth to plunder her own, thrusting and caressing in a mind-blowingly sensual dance.

When he finally broke it off, Brody stared down at her, his heart thumping against her arm, his breathing as ragged as hers.

As if realizing what he'd just done, he all but dropped her to the ground.

Unprepared for the sudden movement, she almost lost her grip on the bottle of Patrón.

Brody cinched his arms around her waist until she steadied, then he stepped away. "I'm sorry. That wasn't supposed to happen." He held up his hands. "I promise it won't happen again."

Stunned speechless, Jessie rubbed the back of her hand across her swollen lips, wondering what just happened. For a moment, she'd forgotten everything, including the fact she had lost her home, job and car that day, and almost dropped a bottle of Patrón that was worth more than she probably had earned that night.

Pulling herself up to her full five feet eight inches, when her knees wanted to buckle, Jessie faked a bravado she certainly didn't feel. "Right. Make sure it doesn't."

He nodded, grabbed the two bottles of Patrón and left her alone in the storeroom.

The whole idea of going to work at the Rafter M Ranch was looking like a huge mistake, but what other choice did she have? She had to limit her mistakes by not kissing one of her bosses. It compromised her ability to think clearly.

"That's right. Don't kiss me again," she whispered through her tingling lips. "Because if you do, I'm likely to throw in the second and third bases. Hell, why not go for a home run?"

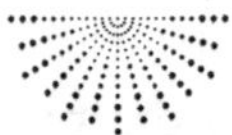

CHAPTER FOUR

*B*rody woke early the next day and crept out of the bed before light. He'd been up late talking with his mother. She'd refused to give in on her demands insisting her boys get on with their lives or she'd sell the ranch and get on with hers. If she'd been on this kick for more than a couple weeks, the two weeks he'd promised Angus might not be enough to convince his mother to change her mind.

He wanted to get to the hunting cabin, dump his gear there and return before the rest of the house woke. If he had to stay longer than two weeks, he couldn't fall behind on his work. He'd put in a call to his agent the previous evening to tell her he'd be in Texas until further notice.

Knowing Sharon, she'd have Dallas galleries lined up to display his efforts within the next couple of weeks. Brody wasn't sure he wanted to display work this close to home. The creative side of him was something he'd never shared with his macho cowboy brothers.

Before moving to Seattle, he'd been equally active on the ranch—training horses, mending fences and the myriad of tasks associated with raising cattle. But he had another side that he didn't tap into until he left behind the Rafter M Ranch.

When he got the call from Colin that his mother was sick, he'd loaded his truck with the items he normally carried out to the Washington coastline—his camera, toolbox, collapsible easel and canvases. Used to painting outside of his studio, it was easy to pack the items in a matter of minutes and hit the road south.

Now, he had to find a place he could set up and leave his things ready for any time he could find to be alone. He wouldn't be home for any longer than it took to convince his mother to back off on her threat to sell the ranch, but he had personal and contractual deadlines he couldn't ignore for any length of time.

Though he'd been away for eight years, he still considered the Rafter M Ranch home. The thought of his mother selling the ranch hit him harder than he'd let on to his brothers. This place held memories of his youth, his father and the happiness of growing up wild and free.

Sure, they'd worked hard next to their father, learning from his example. But they'd had time to ride like the wind, swim in the creek and make forts out of the tumbleweeds that blew in from West Texas.

If his mother sold the place, all he would have were faded memories and no place to come home to.

Brody stepped out onto the porch. The stars still shone bright overhead, with only the faintest gray light appearing on the eastern horizon. He'd have to hurry if he wanted to unload his supplies and get back before the others woke. Brody tiptoed down the steps and climbed into his pickup.

Holding his breath, he cranked the truck's engine and drove, without his headlights, around to the back of the house where the barn stood. Brody shifted into Park, got out, opened the gate to the north pasture and drove his truck through. There weren't any cows close by, but he stopped to close the gate, just in case.

After fifteen minutes of driving slowly over the bumpy dirt road, he arrived at the hunting cabin his grandfather had built fifty years ago. For a long moment, he stared through the windshield. The building was solid and had been structurally maintained, but could use a coat of paint to preserve the exterior wood siding.

With a sigh, Brody dropped down from the truck, carried a battery-powered lantern inside and switched it on, chasing back the majority of shadows.

A coat of dust covered every surface, including the dust cover draped over the old mattress on the iron bed in the corner. Thankfully, the ceiling showed no signs of roof leakage. The building would suffice to store his supplies and he'd work outdoors, taking advantage of the long summer days.

Unloading his truck, he set up his easel and stacked canvases against the wall. It didn't take long, and then he was back in his truck, headed to the ranch house and a hearty breakfast made by the new ranch cook.

Jessie.

He still had doubts about bringing the woman on board at the Rafter M Ranch.

The night before, Brody had stood back while his brothers made a big production of loading Jessie's horse, Scout, into the trailer and tying him off inside to keep him from hurting himself.

"Damned ugly horse," Brody had muttered for the third time, convinced eating three meals a day at the diner in Temptation would be less complicated than hiring Jessie Taylor as the ranch cook.

When Audrey had given her the all clear to leave, Jessie had changed out of the soft-leather dress into her jeans and T-shirt. Even though her legs had been covered in denim, he could still picture the smooth skin and toned muscles.

Jessie had supervised the whole loading process, concerned more for her horse than for herself.

Angus had offered to let her sit in the front seat of the truck, but she'd insisted on taking a rear seat, to be closer to the trailer. Brody hurriedly had climbed in next to her to keep Colin from claiming the spot.

His mother had welcomed her like the daughter she never had, ushering her through the door and upstairs to the guest bedroom beside the master suite.

Exhausted, Brody had cornered his mother when she came down. After their brief, and frustrating, conversation, he'd hit the shower and gone straight to bed. He hadn't seen or heard from Jessie since.

His stomach growled as he parked his truck at the back of the house and climbed down, sniffing the air for the scent of frying bacon. He hoped Jessie was up cooking breakfast, though he didn't smell anything.

Gray light crept across the sky as he let himself in through the back door leading into the kitchen.

The lights were off and nothing was on the stove or in the oven. He found no sign of Jessie or anyone else.

Angus padded barefoot into the kitchen wearing jeans and a T-shirt. He stretched and yawned before asking, "Where's Jessie? I thought she'd be up making breakfast by now."

"I don't know."

Angus frowned. "You're up early. Isn't it still four thirty in the morning in Seattle?"

Brody shrugged. "I slept enough."

Colin appeared behind Angus. "What's for breakfast?" He ran a hand through his hair and craned his neck to see around his brother. "Where's Jessie?"

"Did anyone bother to tell her what time we have breakfast around here?" Brody asked.

Angus glanced at Colin. "I didn't, did you?"

Colin shook his head. "No."

"She went to bed as soon as we got home," Brody said.

"I'll go knock on her door and let her know we're ready for food." Colin started for the stairs.

"I'll take care of it. Between the two of you, you ought to be able to figure out the coffeemaker."

Brody took the stairs two at a time, hurried down the hallway to the guest bedroom and knocked firmly three times.

Nothing stirred behind the door; no sounds came from within. Perhaps she was a heavy sleeper. He knocked again.

The door to the master suite opened and his mother emerged wearing her bathrobe and blinking sleep from her eyes. "What's all the commotion?"

"Just waking Jessie to start breakfast."

"She's a quiet sleeper. After she showered, I didn't hear a peep out of her all night." His mother covered her mouth as she yawned. "Want me to check on her?"

"Please." Brody stepped to the side.

Maggie McFarlan knocked and called out, "Jessie, honey, it's time to get up."

She twisted the doorknob and pushed the door open. "Jessie?"

Brody stepped past his mother into the room. The bed was neatly made, as if it hadn't been slept in. What few clothes she'd brought with her hung neatly in the closet, but there was no sign of Jessie.

"What the hell?" If she hadn't slept in her room, where the hell had she slept?

He went back down the stairs to the main level and checked the living room. Empty.

Angus and Colin met him at the kitchen door. "Is she getting up?"

Brody frowned. "She never went to sleep in her room and she's not in the house."

As one, the three of them looked at each other.

"The barn," Brody said. "She was more worried about her horse than herself."

"I'll get my boots." Angus left the kitchen.

"Me too." Colin followed his older brother.

Brody didn't wait. He left the house and jogged to the barn.

Once inside, he flipped the light switch on the wall and crossed to the stall where they'd taken Scout. He peered over the gate and didn't see anything but the brindle-colored horse. Then a movement directly below him caught his attention.

Jessie lay curled on a tattered horse blanket laid over a pile of straw. Her hair had escaped her ponytail and spread out over the blanket, with a few pieces of straw caught in the strands.

For a long moment Brody took in the image of the fresh-faced woman, her skin softly tanned, dark eyelashes making shadowy crescents on her cheeks. For a tall woman with enough grit to punch him in the face, she appeared vulnerable and lonely, lying in the stall with the only friend she had. Her horse.

Footsteps pounded toward the barn, shaking Brody from the trance.

He opened the door to the stall and bent to touch Jessie's shoulder. "Hey."

Her eyes blinked open and she smiled up at him, her first unguarded smile and it practically lit the inside of the barn, filling Brody's chest with a warmth he hadn't felt in a very long time.

"Hey," she said, her voice like smooth gravel. "What time is it?" She stretched her long arms and legs, pulling the shirt she wore tight over her breasts.

"Six thirty."

"Oh!" Her eyes widened and she sat up. "I meant to be up and cooking by now."

She jumped to her feet, tripped on the blanket and pitched forward into Brody's arms.

He caught her and held her steady until she got her boot free of the blanket. With her hands planted against his chest, she glanced up, her lips soft from sleep and more temptation than Brody could stand.

Despite the promise he'd made the previous night, he bent to capture those lips.

The barn door slammed open. "Brody, did you find her?" Angus called out.

Jessie pushed away from him and straightened her shirt.

"She's here," Brody responded, reaching out to pluck the straw from her hair.

"I'm so sorry. I had every intention of being up first to start breakfast. Just let me wash up and I'll get right to it." She hurried past Brody, Angus and Colin and headed for the house.

The men stood still for a moment, their gazes following the woman.

"Where did you find her?" Colin asked.

"Asleep in the stall with her horse." Brody shook his head.

"I wonder why she didn't feel comfortable in the house," Angus said.

"I think she was more concerned about her horse adapting to a new environment than she was." Colin chuckled. "She's a strange one."

Brody agreed. They knew so little about where she'd come from and why she'd shown up at the Ugly Stick Saloon on a horse with only a few things to call her own. For all they knew, she could be a criminal on the run and they'd invited her into their home without any kind of background check.

"We might as well take care of the animals before breakfast, seeing as Jessie hasn't even started it yet."

Angus grabbed a bucket and filled it with feed. Colin separated several sections of hay and distributed it among the horses in the stalls. Brody headed out to feed the chickens and hogs, the motions natural, like eight years hadn't passed since he'd done the same chores. The only difference was the woman added to the mix. The image of her lying in the stall, sleeping peacefully, with her hair almost the same color of the straw, resonated in his mind.

His fingers itched to get to his paints, but that would have to wait until he could slip away.

JESSIE RACED INTO THE KITCHEN, her heart pounding, not from running but from almost kissing Brody, her new boss. Hell, maybe Imelda had it right and she was a hussy looking to attack the men around her. Only it wasn't all the men. Angus and Colin were every bit as handsome as Brody, but Jessie saw something different in Brody's eyes that she didn't see in Angus's or Colin's. They were brothers—all tall, breathtakingly handsome and rugged the way Jessie preferred men.

But Brody, with those brooding, dangerous looks...wow.

When he'd woken her in the barn, she'd fallen into his arms and practically kissed him.

Jessie pressed her hands to her heated cheeks and hurried upstairs to the bathroom where she splashed water on her face and washed her hands. One look in the mirror made her groan. Her hair stuck out and had straw mixed in with it. Some impression she was making. Late to work her first day on the job, looking like a scarecrow.

She ran to her room, jerked a brush through her hair and secured it with a ponytail. Then she hurried down to the kitchen, anxious to get started. Three hungry men wouldn't be very patient.

After banging around in all the cabinets, she located a couple of skillets, some pancake mix and a mixing bowl. The refrigerator held a dozen eggs and a half a gallon of milk. Surely she could whip up something to get by until she got more familiar with the kitchen and cooking on anything other than a grill. The ranch where her father had been foreman had a cook who specialized in providing meals for a dozen hungry men.

Jessie hadn't learned to cook eggs until her father passed away and she'd been forced to find other accommodations. Even then, working in a boarding stable, living in the office, she'd had only a hot plate to cook on and ended up making sandwiches for practically every meal or heating soup.

How hard could it be to make breakfast for the five of them? All she had to do was follow the directions on the back of the pancake-mix box. Right?

She mixed the ingredients for a batch of pancakes and poured some into the skillet. So far, so good.

Jessie turned on the burner and flames leaped up beneath the pan.

Pancakes cooking, she turned to the rest of the eggs in the carton and cracked them into a bowl, fishing out the fragments of shells that had found their way into the mix. The fragrant scent of pancakes cooking filled the air.

By the time she had all of the eggs in the bowl, something tickled her nose, and then stung her nose, and she turned toward the stove where smoke billowed from the skillet.

"Crap!" Jessie fanned the smoke, trying to get to the pan to remove the burning pancake.

Her eyes stinging so badly she could barely keep them open, Jessie managed to turn off the burner and remove the pan from the stove. With the pan still hot, the pancake continued to burn.

"Damn, damn, damn!"

She grabbed the pan, shoved it beneath the kitchen faucet and turned on the water. Steam mixed with the smoke filling the kitchen. Jessie reached over the sink and opened the window, grabbed a dishtowel and started fanning to help remove the smoke from the kitchen before the men returned to the house and the disaster she'd created.

"Oh dear."

Jessie spun.

Mrs. McFarlan stood behind her.

Between the smoke and her failed attempt at cooking pancakes for the men, Jessie's eyes filled. Damn it, she wasn't going to cry. Her father would be so disappointed. He'd always thought she could handle anything if she set her mind to it.

Mrs. McFarlan glanced out the window. "Too late to cover. You'll have to make do with what you have, and quickly. The boys are on their way back to the house in a hurry. I imagine they saw, or smelled, the smoke."

"What should I do?"

"Get those eggs on the stove and put some toast in the toaster."

Jessie rushed to pour the eggs into a clean skillet. As she tipped the bowl, Mrs. McFarlan cleared her throat. Jessie stopped short of the eggs hitting the pan. "What am I doing wrong?"

"You need to coat the pan with cooking spray or you'll never get the eggs off the bottom."

"Where is it?" Jessie glanced around the kitchen.

"In the cabinet about the stove." Mrs. McFarlan pointed.

Her heart thumping, Jessie jerked open the door and grabbed a can marked *Cooking Spray* and sprayed a healthy amount into the bottom of the pan. Then she dumped the eggs in and turned on the burner.

"Lower the heat or they'll burn. Stay on them, turning the eggs with a spatula until they're done."

Jessie shot the older woman a grateful glance and did as she was instructed.

"Don't forget to pop the toast in the toaster. I gotta go." Mrs. McFarlan backed out of the kitchen as the back door burst open, and the three men charged in.

"Where's the fire?" Colin demanded, swiping at the air with his arm.

Angus was next in the door. He coughed and glanced around the room. "Should I get the fire extinguisher?"

Brody was last in the door. "Please tell me that wasn't our breakfast."

Jessie smiled and pushed the eggs around in the pan, careful not to burn them. "No, no. I'm making scrambled eggs and toast."

"Then why is the house filled with smoke?"

Forcing a confidence she didn't feel, Jessie nodded toward the pan in the sink. "I'm getting used to the gas stove. The pancakes were casualties. I'm used to cooking on an electric burner." There, that wasn't a lie and hopefully they'd give her a chance to prove she could do this job. She didn't have a better offer and doubted she'd find anywhere else that would hire her and board her horse.

Her muscles bunched, breath held, Jessie waited for the men to declare her a failure and ask her to leave. "Why don't y'all wash up? I'll have the eggs on the table when you get back."

Angus and Colin left the room. Brody found a

doorstop and propped the back door open. Then he crossed to the stove where she was standing and leaned close.

Her pulse pounding in her ears, Jessie could feel the heat from Brody's body. She swayed, her body naturally gravitating toward this McFarlan brother. Would he take the opportunity, with the others out of the kitchen, to kiss her?

Brody reached above her and switched on the fan over the stove. "That should help draw the smoke from the room," he said, his breath stirring the loose hairs around her ears.

A shiver slipped across her skin and she drew in a steadying breath. *Don't be silly, Jessie.* It wasn't like the man intended to kiss her. Deep down, she half hoped he would.

He leaned close, his lips brushing against her earlobe. "You don't know how to cook, do you?" he whispered.

The brush of his lips rattled her brain and it took a couple seconds for his words to sink in.

Jessie spun to face him. Her breasts bumped into his chest and she momentarily lost her ability to form a coherent thought. *Sweet Jesus! Why did he have to be so damned sexy?* Scrambling for something to say, she choked out, "I know how to cook."

"Oh yeah. Then why the burned pancakes? And don't tell me it's because of a gas, versus electric, stove."

"I can cook," she maintained.

"What was your last job?" he fired at her so fast she didn't have time to think up a lie.

"I worked with horses at a stable."

"And before that?"

"With horses and cattle on a working ranch."

"And when did you learn to cook?"

He stared hard at her until she caved. "Okay, so I can cook on a grill and an electric hot plate. But how hard can it be to learn? I swear I can do it. I'll prove it to you." She pressed her hands to his chest, the spatula almost whacking him in the face. "Don't fire me on my first day. Please."

He hesitated for a long time.

Jessie's heart slipped to her knees. She'd be riding out before noon, looking for another job and another home for her and Scout.

"I'll give you until the end of the week. But I can't vouch for my brothers."

Jessie let go of the breath she'd been holding and flung her arms around his neck. "Thank you." Her face was so close to his she could feel the warmth of his breath on her lips.

Brody leaned forward, his lips hovering over hers. Then he closed his eyes and set her away from him. "I promised I wouldn't kiss you." He nodded toward the pan on the stove. "You're burning the eggs."

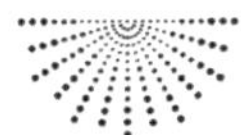

$\mathcal{A}$fter a few days of charred breakfasts with overcooked eggs and burned toast, Brody helped Angus muck the stalls. Colin always left right after breakfast.

"Where's he going?" Brody asked that first morning.

"Colin's built a reputation as a construction contractor. He's got several contracts in the tricounty area. He was planning on building his own house on the ranch before Mom went crazy with her ultimatum. That's on hold now until she settles down."

"He was always good at building things."

Angus chuckled. "Unlike you. You were all thumbs with a hammer."

"Still am."

THE THIRD MORNING HOME, Brody was mucking stalls with Angus. He nodded toward the other stalls. "Mom says you're doing well with your horse breeding program."

"I've been building the Rafter M Ranch name in horse breeding and stud service. Every year, I add either a mare or stallion or purchase semen from some of the top breeders in the country."

"Mom's decision to sell will put a big kink in your operation, won't it?"

"I don't have the kind of money it would take to purchase this ranch or even a fraction of it. Colin and I talked about it. If we put every dollar of our savings together, we might have enough for a down payment on the house, barn and only a hundred acres. The rest would be sold."

"I can't believe she'd sell. But every time I've brought it up, she insists that's exactly what she'll do. She has to be bluffing." Brody shoveled hay and dung into a wheelbarrow.

"She had a Dallas real estate broker out to give her an idea of what it would go for. I thought she was kidding too, but she's been looking at brochures of retirement communities in Florida. She said she's ready for a change and if that change doesn't include daughters-in-law and grandchildren, she's done with the ranch."

"I have no plans to marry and settle down. This is emotional blackmail, the way I see it."

Angus dumped a load of muck into his own wheelbarrow and leaned on his hay rake. "It's her property."

Brody dug the rake into soiled straw in the stall he worked. "We grew up here. We ought to have a say."

"She can do anything she wants with it. Her signature is all that's needed on sales documents."

"I guess after living here thirty-five years, she's tired of it."

"And tired of taking care of us," Angus said. "Sorry you walked into that. It isn't like she's been cooking for you the past eight years. Colin and I didn't appreciate all she did for us until she stopped doing it."

"I can't say much. I ate out or had food delivered. I can open a can of soup and make a sandwich, but that's the extent of my cooking skills."

Angus grinned. "I'm thinking that's about the extent of Jessie's skills as well."

Brody's lips pressed together at the same time as his body fired up. If he were smart, he'd let her go now and cut his losses. But the plea in her gray-blue eyes, and seeing her sleeping in the stall that first morning with Scout, had touched him more than he cared to admit. If they fired her, she had nowhere else to go.

The woman might be hopeless in the kitchen, but she had proven useful with the animals and ranch work. Brody was quickly getting used to seeing her tall, lithe form around the place. He found himself looking for her around every corner inside the house and around the outbuildings. Occasionally he bumped into her and that spark of electricity reminded him of that first kiss, making him want to repeat it over and over again. "I gave her until the end of the week to improve the cooking."

"Hopefully she will pick up before we starve." Angus

lifted the handles of his wheelbarrow and pushed it out the back door of the barn, to the compost pile.

Brody followed. Engine noise caught his attention and he walked to the edge of the barn. His mother's SUV pulled out of the driveway with Jessie in the passenger seat.

Angus draped an arm over Brody' shoulder and shook his head. "I don't think we'd be able to fire the girl now, even if we wanted. Mom's already attached to her." He raised his hands. "I'm already taken, so it'll be interesting to see who she tries to match her with, you or Colin. Come to think of it, I wonder if she's taking her by one of Colin's worksites to show off what he's capable of. You know, good boyfriend or husband material."

Brody's muscles bunched at the thought of Jessie with Colin. Hell, he'd seen her first. Then he had to remind himself that he wasn't in the market for a wife or relationship of any kind. He was headed back to Seattle as soon as his mother let go of the crazy notion of selling the ranch.

"Good for Mom. Two out of three of her sons married off might satisfy her." He glanced down at the wheelbarrow. "Are we done in the barn?"

"I am. I have horses to exercise. I won't need any help if you have something else to do."

"I need a few items from town. I think I'll go take care of that. If you need me this afternoon, I should be back after lunch."

Angus chuckled. "You might want to eat lunch while you're in town. Do it out of self-preservation."

Brody hurried to the house, showered and changed into clean jeans and boots and headed for town, telling himself he really did need some personal items and maybe a can of paint thinner. He wasn't going after Jessie to see if his mother was taking her to visit one of Colin's jobsites.

Besides, Jessie might not be interested in his brother. Brody wondered if she'd felt that spark of electricity when she'd fallen into his arms in the storeroom of the Ugly Stick Saloon. When he'd kissed her, she sure as hell kissed him back. In the barn the other morning, he'd been tempted to break his promise and kiss her again, and nearly did in the kitchen when she'd burned their breakfast.

What was wrong with him? He barely knew the girl and she wasn't even his type. That girl-next-door, tough gal might appeal to some, but it didn't appeal to him. He liked girls who knew they were girls and didn't try to be all macho.

Like Fancy?

Yeah, and look where that had gotten him. He'd lost his girl and his brother in that relationship.

Brody was headed back to Seattle as soon as possible. He'd do nobody any favors by getting involved with someone who was more at home on a ranch in Texas than anywhere else in the world.

"THANK you for taking me grocery shopping, Mrs. McFarlan. I wouldn't have the first clue what to buy, or the money to buy it."

"I'm along for the company. Don't you let the boys know I'm shopping for them. And since you don't have a vehicle or access to the ranch bank account, someone had to take you."

"I really do appreciate your help that first morning. I didn't make a good first impression. And I can't keep making peanut butter and jelly sandwiches or grilling burgers, like I have for the past couple days. I have to make a real dinner tonight, or I'll be out job hunting again."

"Don't you worry. I have a few recipes you can follow. It just takes a little patience and attention to what's on the fire. Didn't your mother teach you to cook anything?"

Jessie shook her head. "My mother left my father when I was four. I barely remember her. Dad raised me the best he could."

"What did he do for a living?"

"He was a ranch foreman for a big ranch in the Panhandle."

"Where is he now?"

Jessie's chest tightened and tears stung her eyes. "He died two years ago of a massive heart attack. No one knew he even had a problem. Especially me." A tear slipped from the corner of her eye and she brushed it away with the back of her hand.

"Same thing happened to my husband. One minute we were one big, happy family. The next he was dead and gone, leaving me and my three sons to manage the ranch he loved so much."

"At least you weren't forced out of the only home

you ever knew."

"Is that what happened to you?"

Jessie nodded. "I worked as one of the ranch hands and lived in the foreman's house with my father."

Mrs. McFarlan shook her head. "And when your father passed away, they hired another foreman and you were out of a place to live?"

"Yeah. I couldn't afford to work at the ranch anymore without a place to live. All I have left of the life I had with my father is the horse he gave me for my twenty-first birthday." She smiled. "The ranch owner didn't want him because he said he was ugly." Her lips pressed together. "He might not be the prettiest color, but he's a damned good horse." And her only friend.

"I'm sure he's a fine horse. And if you want to help out on the ranch, I'm sure the boys will appreciate your efforts."

As they entered Temptation, Jessie looked around eagerly, anxious to get to know the town she could be calling home if all went well with her job at the ranch. It was quaint, with one stoplight, a decent-sized grocery store, a dress shop, beauty shop, flower shop and diner.

"I thought we might stop at a little clothing store, then eat lunch at the diner and finish off by purchasing groceries."

"You're driving, even though you say you're only along for the ride," Jessie said.

THE CLOTHING STORE on Main Street had a nice variety

of women's clothing, including shorts, tops, dresses and jeans.

Mrs. McFarlan headed straight for the rack of short party dresses and thumbed through them until she found a pale-blue one. She held it up to Jessie and smiled. "This one brings the color out in your eyes. You should try it on."

Jessie shook her head. "I can't afford any new clothes. I only just started working for the Rafter M Ranch. I haven't even drawn my first paycheck." Her eyes widened. "You didn't come in here on my account, did you?" She backed toward the door. "I don't have much, ma'am, but what I have, I paid for myself."

"Honey, from what I can tell, you only have the jeans you're wearing and one other pair. You need more than that."

"I have all I need." Jessie spun and headed for the door. "I'll just wait outside until you're done shopping in here."

Her cheeks heated, Jessie stepped out onto the sidewalk, her heart pounding and her eyes burning. God, she hated when people pitied her and thought she was a charity case. Damn it, she could take care of herself. She didn't need handouts. She'd work for what she had, by God.

Mrs. McFarlan stepped out of the shop and slipped an arm around Jessie's waist. "Please accept my apologies. I only want to help."

"Thank you, but I don't need anything I haven't earned."

"Everyone needs a little help every once in a while.

It's not a poor reflection on you if you let someone give you a hand. You could consider it a hand up, not a handout."

"I'd rather not consider it at all, thank you." Jessie forced a smile. "If my clothes bother you that much, perhaps there's a thrift store around here? I have a little money I earned working at the Ugly Stick Saloon."

Mrs. McFarlan grinned. "As a matter of fact, there is. Follow me."

She led her to a store one block off Main Street that sold clothes to raise money for the local women's shelter. "Not only will you be getting a bargain on what you buy, but your money will go toward helping out women who are in dire situations."

Jessie searched through the clothes racks and selected three pairs of gently worn jeans in her size and a couple of tops. Mrs. McFarlan found a dress similar to the one in the other store, in a heather blue, and held it out to her.

"I have no need for a dress," Jessie said. "The only one I ever owned was the one I wore to my father's funeral. I gave it to the Salvation Army before I left the ranch my father gave his life to."

"Let me buy this one for you. It's not a dress to wear to a funeral and it would be nice to have in case you go dancing."

"Ma'am, I really don't see a need for it, and I won't take your money." Jessie placed her things on the counter.

The clerk glanced at the dress. "That color would go perfectly with your eyes and it's marked down for clearance." She turned over the price tag and it was so ridiculously low—and Mrs. McFarlan really wanted her to have a dress—that Jessie said, "Okay, I'll take it, these tops and the jeans."

"You're in luck on the jeans too. Today all denim is fifty percent off the marked prices."

"Then you can afford this one too." Mrs. McFarlan laid another dress on the counter.

The clerk smiled. "That one was marked down today too."

Giving in to Mrs. M's desire to see her in dresses, Jessie nodded.

The woman rang up her purchases and Jessie was happy to see that she'd barely put a dent in the little bit of money she'd earned.

With new-to-her clothes and money in her pocket, she left the store with a smile on her face.

"That was fun," Mrs. McFarlan said, hooking her purchase of a like-new designer purse on her arm. "I'll have to remember to shop there more often."

The smell of fried chicken and fresh bread drifted to Jessie from the diner a block down Main Street and her stomach grumbled. "Didn't you say you wanted to have lunch before the grocery store?"

Mrs. McFarlan grinned. "Yes, I did."

"Good, because I can afford it and I'm hungry."

"Great. So am I."

MRS. MCFARLAN LED the way into the diner.

As Jessie stepped through the doorway, the older

woman stopped abruptly and her cheeks turned a soft shade of pink.

"Mrs. McFarlan, are you all right?" Jessie asked.

"Oh my." She pressed a hand to her chest. "That man looks even better than he did in high school."

"What man?" Jessie glanced around the diner.

Her gaze captured by a gorgeous, silver-haired man standing at the cash register, smiling as he handed the cashier some cash. He winked and told her to keep the change. Then he turned toward a younger woman with shimmering auburn hair and bright-green eyes and offered her his arm. That the man had a young woman on his arm didn't seem to faze Mrs. M as she stood transfixed, barely through the door of the diner.

As the man approached, he smiled at Mrs. M and then did a double take. "Maggie? Maggie Smith?"

He dropped the arm of the auburn-haired beauty and took both of Mrs. M's hands in his. "You look exactly the same as you did back in high school. It's so very nice to see you again. Hell, seeing you brings back some fond memories."

"Oh, go on." Maggie blushed and batted her eyes. "It's good to see you too, Carl. Are you in town on a visit?"

He grinned and drew the woman with the auburn hair up beside him. "Not actually a visit. I've retired from the corporate world and bought the old Frazier place on the river."

Mrs. M's eyes rounded. "Really? I thought that old house was falling down."

"It is. But it's livable until I can have a new house

built. I don't suppose you know a trustworthy contractor in the area?"

"As a matter of fact, my son Colin is an up-and-coming contractor making quite a name for himself."

"How is Colin?" the young woman spoke for the first time.

"I'm sorry." Carl turned to his companion. "This is my real estate agent, Fancy Wilson. I'm her first big sale since she returned to Temptation."

Mrs. M's smile tightened, and she hesitated before holding out her hand to the young woman. "Fancy. Yes, I remember you. You and Brody were engaged briefly, eight years ago. I'm sorry I didn't get to know you better. That was the year my husband passed."

Jessie's heart hit the bottom of her belly. This beauty had been engaged to Brody McFarlan? Holy hell. What could possibly have happened to make him break it off with her? She was stunningly gorgeous. Everything a man could want in a woman. Jessie felt positively gawky and manly in her presence.

"Nice to see you, Mrs. McFarlan." Even the woman's voice was like melted chocolate, seeping into her ears.

The more Jessie was near her, the more inadequate she felt.

Mrs. M let go of Fancy's hand. "Brody never told me why you two broke it off, and he moved shortly afterward, so I never got the story. I hope it was a mutual agreement."

She nodded. "More or less. We were so young anyway. It was just as well." Fancy smiled, the light not quite reaching her eyes.

Mrs. M turned to Jessie. "Carl, this is Jessie Taylor. She's staying with us at the Rafter M Ranch."

"It is always my pleasure to meet a lovely young lady." Carl turned his smile on Jessie and made her blush almost as much as Mrs. M.

"Nice to meet you," Jessie murmured.

"I'm looking forward to reconnecting with my old hometown," Carl said.

"We were about to have lunch, if you'd like to join us," Mrs. M offered.

Carl shook his head. "I'm sorry, we just finished eating, and I have business at the bank."

Fancy smiled. "And I'm headed over to the salon to have my hair styled."

"Thank you for the invitation, though." Carl lifted Mrs. M's hand again and gave her a smile that melted even Jessie's knees. "I do want to catch up with you, Maggie. I don't suppose you'd have dinner with me tonight?"

Again, Mrs. M's cheeks blossomed a pretty pink, and she glanced down at her hand in his. "That would be nice. I'd like that."

"I'll pick you up at seven."

"No need. It's such a long drive out to the ranch." Maggie smiled up at the man. "I could meet you in town."

"Nonsense. I'd love to drive out and see what you and your boys have done with the Rafter M Ranch. I heard your oldest son is raising horses. I might be interested in purchasing some for my place, when I've had a chance to renovate the old barn to make it safe."

"Well then, tonight I'd be happy to give you a tour," Maggie said.

The door opened behind them and Jessie moved to allow the person room to enter. When she turned, she found Colin beside her, his gaze riveted on Fancy.

Fancy's cheeks blanched and she caught her full, lush bottom lip between her teeth.

"Colin, honey, you remember Fancy Wilson. She just sold the old Frazier place to Carl." Maggie waved him forward. "Carl, this is my son Colin. He's the one who's in construction."

The youngest McFarlan brother appeared to be frozen in the middle of the open doorway. After a moment he shook himself and stepped forward to shake Carl's hand. When he turned to take Fancy's, a muscle twitched in his jaw. "Fancy."

She looked up at him and then lowered her eyelids, hiding the expression in her green eyes.

Jessie was better at reading horses than people, but it was obvious there was something going on between Colin and Fancy.

The door opened again.

Jessie's body tensed and she sensed Brody standing behind her. With a steadying breath, she turned.

They'd pointedly avoided each other for the past few days, though it was difficult, living under the same roof. Every time Brody was in the same room as Jessie, heat sizzled through her, reminding her of his first kiss. Now, as he stood close enough to touch, she swayed toward him like metal to a magnet.

His gaze captured hers. "Jessie, I didn't expect to find you here."

At that moment, Colin stepped to the side.

Brody looked past his mother to his younger brother, his eyes narrowing ever so slightly. Then his gaze shifted to the woman standing beside Colin and his brows furrowed.

"Carl, this is my middle son, Brody," Mrs. M said. "Brody, this is Carl Landers."

The fierce frown disappeared and all expression was wiped from Brody's face as he extended a hand to Mr. Landers. "Mr. Landers. Nice to meet you." He turned to Fancy and nodded. "Fancy." Without sparing any more than the brief acknowledgment, he faced his mother. "I'm headed to the hardware store. Do you need any supplies?"

Maggie McFarlan shook her head. "Not that I can think of."

With a glance at Carl, Brody exited the diner, leaving a painful silence in his wake.

Jessie stared after him.

Brody walked away, his posture stiff, his hands fisted at his sides.

When he disappeared past the windows, Jessie turned to the people standing in the restaurant.

Colin exchanged a look with Fancy. "It's nice to see you. I'd better get back to work."

"Aren't you going to join us for lunch?" his mother asked.

Colin gave his mother a tight smile and shook his

head. "Not today." He nodded to Carl and glanced one last time at Fancy before he left the diner.

Maggie shrugged. "I guess it's just you and me, Jessie."

"See you tonight." Carl waved and escorted his real estate agent to the door.

The McFarlan matron found a seat in a booth and sighed.

Jessie settled across from her, reluctant to say anything about what just happened, wondering what lunch would have been like had Brody stayed.

Mrs. M wasn't so reticent. "Did you feel the tension in the air when Colin and Brody came in? Or was it just me?"

"I felt it," Jessie responded. "It's none of my business, but it seemed to revolve around Fancy."

"I believe it's the reason Brody let the Rafter M Ranch in the first place." The older woman's eyes narrowed. "I'd also bet whatever happened between the three of them caused Brody and Fancy to break off their engagement."

Jessie's chest tightened. The shock and anger on Brody's face could mean only one thing. He still had feelings for his ex-fiancée. Not that it should bother her, and it wouldn't have if he hadn't kissed her.

"I wish I'd been more involved back then," Mrs. M said, breaking through Jessie's thoughts.

"Sounds like you were going through hard times. I'm sorry you lost your husband."

"I loved him dearly." Maggie's eyes misted. "He and Carl were friends back in high school." She smiled. "If I hadn't fallen in love with John—who knows?—I might have married Carl instead."

"He seemed very nice."

Maggie sighed. "He's even more handsome than he was when we were teens."

"You should enjoy your date with him tonight."

"Date?" Maggie shook her head, staring at Jessie as if she'd said something odd. "He just wants to catch up with an old friend." She chuckled. "Date? I'm too old to date."

"Mrs. M, you're never too old to date. I mean, look at you. You're a beautiful woman." Jessie grinned. "I'm no expert on dating, but if he's picking you up at the ranch, I'd call that a date."

Mrs. M's cheeks flushed a bright pink. "Me, on a date? With Carl the Heartbreaker?" She fanned herself. "That's what they called him in high school. He left a trail of broken female hearts."

"Including yours?"

She waved her hand. "Heavens no. I loved my John from the moment we met and I'll miss him until I die."

Jessie covered her hand. "But you have the rest of your life to live. Surely he wouldn't have wanted you to live it alone."

"No. He would want me to move on." Mrs. M glanced up. "I wasn't ready until recently." She giggled like a schoolgirl. "I have a date."

Happy for Mrs. M, Jessie sat back, ordered the lunch special of fried chicken and homemade bread rolls and thought back over the meeting between Colin, Fancy and Brody. Sadly, she suspected a love triangle. From the frigid glances the brothers had exchanged, they weren't over it or their anger toward each other.

At least it did one thing. It took Jessie out of the equation. If Brody still loved Fancy, now that she was back in town he wouldn't have eyes for anyone else.

There would be no more stolen kisses.

When she should have been happy about that, she was left with an emptiness in her chest, and she lost her appetite for the wonderful chicken cooked by the best chef in Temptation.

CHAPTER SIX

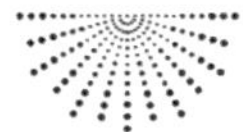

*B*rody floored the accelerator all the way back to the ranch and didn't stop there.

Angus was out hooking up mares to the exercise walker when Brody opened the gate, drove through and closed it behind him. He didn't want to stop and chat with his older brother. He had nothing to say. Fancy was back in town and Colin had already sniffed her out.

Not until he'd reached the cabin did Brody stop and analyze how he'd felt when he walked into that diner.

His first reaction had been the swell of excitement at catching Jessie in town, followed by a sharp stab of jealousy when he'd seen Colin had beat him to her.

When Fancy came into view, the old anger and resentment resurfaced like heated lava through a narrow vent. Had Colin decided he wanted both women? Was it his way of taking away anything Brody might want?

As he climbed down from his SUV, he paused. Fancy

had been even more beautiful than he remembered from the last time he'd seen her eight years ago. But it was Jessie he thought of now. Her tall, lithe figure, the hay-colored, silky hair pulled back in a ponytail and the love she had for a horse so ugly Brody was surprised Angus allowed her to keep him in the barn alongside the prize mares of his breeding program.

In the few short days he'd known her, Jessie, the cook who burned everything, had thrown a punch knocking him flat on his ass and wiggled her way into his conscious and subconscious thoughts. Though he'd made it his mission to avoid her, Brody managed to bump into her every time he turned around. And he found Jessie to be more real and desirable to him than a dozen Fancys.

He grabbed the can of paint thinner from the sack on the back floorboard of his truck and hurried into the hunting cabin. Within minutes, he'd set up his easel outside in the sunshine, squirt globs of oil paint on his palette and jabbed his paintbrush into the rich colors. Channeling all his frustration, he slashed paint onto a blank canvas in bold strokes. All the anger he'd felt over the eight years he'd been gone funneled through his fingers, through the brush and onto the canvas.

For several hours, he focused on his work, ignoring everything else around him. When he touched the last dab of paint onto the picture, he let go of the tension and stepped back.

"I didn't realize you were so good," a voice said over his shoulder.

Angus stood a few feet behind him, holding the reins of a palomino mare.

Brody stepped in front of the canvas to block his brother's view of something so personal he'd never shared it with his family.

"Please. Let me see." Angus tied the mare's reins to the hitching post in front of the cabin, stepped around Brody and stared at the painting of a brindle horse, rearing on a windblown, grassy knoll, storm clouds billowing in the background. In front of the horse stood a young woman with long, straight blonde hair, wearing jeans and cowboy boots, her back to the viewer, her arm raised as if to gentle the animal.

As Brody really looked at the painting, he realized nowhere in the composition was Colin or Fancy.

"You even made Scout look amazing." Angus turned to Brody. "Is this what you've been doing in Seattle? Painting?"

Still too wound up from the outpouring of emotion he invariably released into his work, Brody shook his head. "I'd rather you didn't say anything to anyone else about this."

Angus's brows knit and he glanced back at the painting. "It's incredible. I feel like the horse could leap off the page, and Jessie... I can see why you don't want to fire her. You've captured something I would feel but couldn't put into words to describe."

"It's just a picture." Brody lifted the easel, painting and all, and carried it into the hunting cabin.

His older brother followed him to the door and

opened his mouth to argue the point. One glance at Brody's face and he shut his mouth.

Closing the cabin door behind him, Brody let the strain of the past few hours roll off his shoulders, as if by painting and then putting the image away, he could compartmentalize his life. "Did you need help with anything?"

"Not today, but tomorrow I could use a hand. The Brangus bull knocked down a portion of the fence north of the swimming hole. It's getting too late to mend it today, and tomorrow I have an appointment at the architectural firm I contract with. I might not be back in time to take care of it."

"I'll handle it." Brody walked to the palomino and rubbed his hand along the animal's neck, hoping to take the focus off his painting. "How's that working for you, owning a horse breeding business and working as a contract architect to one of the largest Dallas-based architectural firms?"

"It's actually working out well. I make great money with the firm. I get to work my own hours doing what I love, and I'm building my breeding program."

Brody scratched behind the horse's ear. "How serious are you about this Gwen woman?" He looked back at his brother. "I mean, Mom's not pushing you into something more than you want, is she?"

"I'm as serious as it gets about Gwen. This whole thing with Mom threatening to sell the ranch has me on hold about taking the next step with Gwen."

"The next step?" Brody's brows rose. "Are you going to propose?"

"I want to marry her before she changes her mind. She's beautiful, intelligent and driven about her work. She loves Dalton, and I think she loves me too. But I don't want to ask her to marry me until I know whether or not I'll have a home to bring them to, or if I'll have to scramble to find a place I can raise my horses. Worst-case scenario, I sell the horses and move to Dallas and go back to work full time with the firm."

His mother's ultimatum weighed heavily on Brody. He wasn't the only one impacted by it. Angus had given up a lot to stay with their mother and run the ranch when their father died. Then when their mother had been diagnosed with cancer he'd been the rock in her life, to see her through surgery and recovery. Brody had more or less run away from his brother's betrayal, from the certainty that Fancy had never loved him and from obligations of being a part of the family. He had a crapload of regret and leaving now would only add to it.

But to marry just to please his mother? He wouldn't go that far.

"Hey…" Angus touched Brody's arm, "…if you don't want to stay, that's your right. Colin and I can figure this out. You have a life and what looks like a tremendous amount of talent. Don't let this old ranch hold you back."

Brody shook his head. "I'm staying until *we* figure this out."

"What about your art?"

"I can paint anywhere."

"Yeah, but don't you need to be closer to a place

where people appreciate fine art? Temptation isn't exactly a cultural Mecca."

"My agent is already working on setting up a gallery exhibit in Dallas." He hoped like hell the art buyers of Texas liked what he painted as much as those in Seattle did; otherwise, he'd be flying back and forth from Texas to Seattle to maintain his sales and that would cut into his time to create.

"I'm glad to hear that." Angus stared at the closed cabin door. "You really should show Mom. She'd be so proud."

"I will," Brody said. "When I'm ready."

JESSIE WORKED ALL AFTERNOON, unloading groceries she and Mrs. M had selected at the store, and then preparing a huge pan of lasagna under the close tutelage of the McFarlan-family matriarch. While Jessie worked, Mrs. M filled her in on the brothers' childhood antics from junior rodeo riding to playing hooky on warm spring days.

"Set the timer for thirty minutes so you don't forget about it," Mrs. M suggested as Jessie slid the casserole dish full of noodles, sauce and cheesy deliciousness into the preheated oven.

Jessie studied the oven controls and set the timer.

"That wasn't so hard, was it?"

With a smile, Jessie turned to Mrs. M. "No, it wasn't."

"And my mama always told me a way to a man's heart is through his stomach."

"I don't want to win their hearts," Jessie said. "I just

want to prove that I can cook. I really need this job."

"As long as you don't burn that lasagna, you'll be on the road to proving yourself. Now, while supper's cooking, why don't you try on that dress I washed and ironed for you? It doesn't hurt for the chef to look as good as the food."

"I don't know." Jessie shrugged. "I've never felt comfortable in a dress. I barely know how to wear one." An image of Brody's ex-fiancée flashed through Jessie's mind. Fancy Wilson had not only looked good in a dress, she'd worn it like a fashion statement.

Mrs. M's brows dipped. "It's amazing what clothes do for your confidence, and how others perceive you. Take Fancy Wilson…"

Jessie would rather not talk about the auburn-haired beauty. "What about her?"

"Put her in a pair of old jeans and a T-shirt and she wouldn't look any different from any other cowgirl in the county."

"I doubt that. I bet she'd look good in anything she wore."

Mrs. M's lips curled. "She got to you, didn't she?"

Jessie turned toward the stovetop, afraid the older woman would see right through her. "I don't know what you're talking about."

"Don't let a pretty piece of fluff like Fancy make you feel any less than beautiful." Mrs. M stood and crossed to Jessie. "I see a beautiful woman in those blue-gray eyes of yours. Wear the dress for me tonight. I think you'll be surprised at how good you look in it. You'll give that Fancy a run for her money."

Her competitive spirit spiked, until she reminded herself out loud, "I'm not in competition with Fancy."

"No?" Mrs. M's smile widened. "Well, we'll just see about that. Oh, and don't set a plate at the table for me. Remember? I'm going out."

Not sure what the woman was up to, Jessie couldn't say no to her. Not after she'd spent her entire afternoon teaching Jessie how to make lasagna. Dinner that night would be edible and might help save her job.

Thirty minutes later, Jessie wore the blue dress. Mrs. McFarlan had helped her do her hair, using a flat iron to smooth out the tangles and kinks from the elastic band. It hung long and straight around her shoulders and halfway down her back. The older woman even insisted on applying a little blush to Jessie's cheeks and adding a smoky shadow to her eyes. By the time Mrs. M finished, Jessie didn't recognize the pretty blonde in the mirror.

She might not be gorgeous enough to compete with the beautiful Fancy, but she looked better than she ever had.

Back in the kitchen as the timer beeped, Jessie couldn't help smiling as she peered through the glass oven door. The guys would be pleased. The lasagna turned out perfect.

Angus and Colin came in through the back door, hung their hats on pegs on the wall and sniffed the air.

"Something smells good enough to eat," Colin said. "What's for dinner?"

"Lasagna." Jessie pulled the lightly browned dish

from the oven and set it on a hot pad. "Go wash up and I'll have it on the table when you're ready."

Both men stopped short as Jessie straightened.

Colin made a show of looking around. "I hear Jessie talking, but I don't see anyone here but one gorgeous blonde in a pretty blue dress."

Angus grinned. "Wow. You look amazing."

Colin stepped up to Jessie, took her hand and twirled her about. "That dress needs to go dancing."

Jessie's cheeks heated and she glanced past the two brothers to the empty doorway. "Is Brody coming?"

Angus's eyes narrowed for a split second, and then he shook his head. "Don't wait on him. He might be late."

"Oh." An unexpected pressure squeezed against Jessie's chest and she turned away, hoping Angus and Colin hadn't seen the disappointment in her face.

The men hurried off to wash up.

By the time they returned, Jessie had the lasagna on the table and a bowl of fresh salad made of vegetables from Mrs. M's garden.

Angus glanced around. "Where's Mom?"

Jessie set a basket full of garlic bread next to the salad. "She's getting ready to go on her date."

Angus stopped with his hand on a chair and frowned. "Date? What date?"

Colin grimaced. "Didn't I mention? She ran into Carl Landers in town."

With a quick headshake, Angus asked, "What does

this Carl Landers have to do with Mom going on a date?"

"Mr. Landers asked your mother out to dinner tonight," Jessie said.

Angus's eyes widened. "And she agreed?"

Jessie nodded.

Colin shrugged. "So?"

"Do you realize they used to call him Heartbreak Carl back when Mom and Dad were in high school?" Angus yanked the chair out from under the table and sat down.

Colin's brows quirked upward. "Again...so? That was over thirty years ago."

"I don't want Mom to get hurt."

Jessie grabbed a spatula and dug into the lasagna, cutting long rectangles of the cheesy, mouthwatering dish, and filled Angus's and Colin's plates. Then she served up the salad in the small bowls beside each man's plate, shaking her head as the men worried over their mother. They probably had a hard time seeing her as anything other than their mother who'd been married to their father. Mrs. McFarlan was first and foremost a woman with a lot of good years left in her.

"We'll just have to keep an eye on them." Angus shoved a forkful of lasagna into his mouth.

"Keep an eye on who?" Mrs. McFarlan appeared in the doorway, looking as trim and pretty as a schoolgirl, wearing a cream-colored dress and low-heeled pumps. Her hair brushed her shoulders and she wore eye makeup, lipstick and a light dusting of blush.

Jessie smiled. "You look wonderful."

"Is the dress too young for an old woman like me?" Mrs. M turned like a model on a runway.

"Not at all," Jessie said. "It's perfect and you're not an old woman. You look young and alive."

The two brothers rose from the table.

Angus scowled. "What's this about you going on a date?"

"I'm having dinner with Carl Landers." Mrs. M took Jessie's hands. "Did my boys compliment the chef?" She cast a stern glance at her sons.

Colin saluted. "The lasagna is great. Tastes a lot like yours, Mom."

She smiled. "Ah, but I didn't cook it. Jessie did." She turned Jessie around. "Colin, did you bother to tell Jessie how pretty she looked in her dress?"

Jessie's cheeks burned. "He mentioned it."

"Mom, she's gorgeous, and I told her." Colin grimaced. "Well, not in so many words."

"Angus?" his mother prompted.

"Jessie, you look great," Angus said and turned to his mother. "Now, what's going on? I've never known you to go on a date. Why the sudden interest?"

His mother tilted her chin. "You and your brothers might think your mother is too old to care about anything other than her sons and this ranch. I'll have you know, I might be older than you, but I want to live and have fun and fall in love again."

"But what about Dad?" Angus said softly.

Mrs. M's lips firmed. "Listen to me." Her brows angled toward the bridge of her nose. "I loved your father more than anyone in this world. When he passed,

I thought I would die with him." She shook her head, her eyes glistening. "But I didn't. It's been eight years. I think he'd agree that I've grieved long enough. Like I've asked you boys to get on with your lives, I'm taking my own advice and getting on with mine."

Jessie's heart squeezed at the emotion in Maggie McFarlan's voice. She glanced at Angus and Colin and almost laughed at the shocked expressions on their faces. She wanted to cheer for the older McFarlan and her fierce desire to join life again instead of sitting on the sidelines.

"What?" Maggie said. "You don't think your mother should have needs and desires?"

Angus covered his ears. "I don't want to hear this."

"I don't know." Colin grinned. "I think Mom deserves to be happy, especially after putting up with us all these years."

"Don't you want me to be happy, Angus?" she asked.

"Of course." Angus took her hands. "And Dad would have wanted you to be happy. I just can't see you with anyone but Dad."

Mrs. M sighed. "Me either. But I can't live in the past. Besides, this is just dinner. I'm not marrying the man."

"But what if you do?" Angus asked.

"We'll cross that bridge if we come to it." She patted her son's cheek. "I'm glad you've found someone who makes you happy. I hope your brothers are as fortunate." Maggie stared at Colin who'd settled in his chair and shoved another forkful of lasagna into his mouth.

"What?" Colin asked.

"Have you done anything about getting on with your life?" she asked.

Colin set his fork down. "Hey, I got Brody here."

"By lying to him." His mother crossed her arms. "I can't believe you told him I was sick."

"He came, didn't he? Proves he still cares about you, even if he doesn't care about the rest of us."

"Give him time." Angus took his seat. "He'll come around."

"I don't know." Colin stared at the wall as if seeing something other than a calendar with the picture of a cow in a field. "With Fancy back in town, he might decide to leave sooner."

"What happened between Brody and Fancy?" Mrs. McFarlan asked. "He never told me."

"She discovered she didn't love him enough to marry him, and called it off before they both made a big mistake." Colin polished off the last bite on his plate, pushed back from the table and stood. "Jessie, good meal. Angus, enjoy it. Mom, I hope you have a nice time out with Mr. Landers. You deserve to be happy." After his little speech, Colin carried his plate to the sink and left the room.

Mrs. McFarlan stared after her son. "Did I say something wrong?"

Angus concentrated on the food in front of him. "Who the heck knows? Colin's had a bug up his butt ever since Brody and Fancy broke it off. He and Brody haven't talked much since."

"You think Colin had something to do with Fancy breaking up with Brody?" Mrs. McFarlan asked.

The way Colin lit up when he saw Fancy today, Jessie wouldn't doubt it. The man had feelings for the pretty lady.

Jessie sighed.

Based on Brody's reaction to seeing Fancy today, Jessie would go so far as to say he wasn't over the woman.

And for a moment in that diner, Jessie had thought Brody was happy to see *her*—Jessie. Boy, had she been wrong. Why she'd been disappointed at the realization, she didn't know. Hell, they'd only known each other a short time.

A knock on the front door shook her out of her musings.

"That will be Carl." Mrs. McFarlan smiled and her cheeks glowed a soft pink. "I feel like a teenager going out on her first date."

Jessie forced a smile for the woman. "You look like a teenager."

"Thank you, dear." She touched Jessie's arm. "Wish one of my boys would see what a lovely young woman you are."

"Oh, ma'am." Jessie raised her hands. "I'm not in the market to marry." She glanced at Angus. "I hope you don't think that's why I signed on."

Angus's lips twisted. "I know why you accepted our offer. You're crazy about that horse of yours. I still can't believe you rode away from your last job with not much more than the clothes on your back."

"Scout was a gift from my father," Jessie whispered. "I would never abandon him."

"Exactly." The oldest McFarlan rose from the table. "Come on, Mom, let me read the Heartbreaker the riot act so that he doesn't go breaking your heart."

"Oh, Angus. Don't be silly. I'm a grown woman."

"Yeah, but you've been out of action for a long time. Things have changed a little." He pointed at Jessie. "I'll be back for my dinner, which, I might say, is great."

Jessie smiled at Angus while Mrs. McFarlan winked at her.

Once Mrs. M left, Jessie sat with Angus and they silently finished their dinner.

"Good job, Jessie. Keep it up and the job will be permanent. I think Mom is enjoying her time off."

"Thanks."

Angus left to make one last pass through the barn.

Jessie cleared the table, changed from sandals to her cowboy boots and went out to check on Scout.

THE HORSE HAD ADJUSTED to his new home better than Jessie.

As the hired help, Jessie didn't know how she fit into the McFarlan family. She was expected to live in the house, but she really didn't feel comfortable living with the family she was supposed to serve.

Her last boss only wanted her to clean the stables and feed the horses. Outside of that, he didn't want to see her. That had been fine with Jessie.

With the McFarlans she'd already learned more than she felt she had a right to. Brody and Colin had an ongoing feud over a woman, Angus was involved with a woman from Dallas, and Mrs. McFarlan hadn't dated since the death of her husband eight years ago. That, and all about the brothers' lives as children.

Her heart skipped several beats. She hadn't felt this close to a family since her father died. God, she missed him.

"Scout, I hope you like it here. I'm trying my best to make it work out." And if the middle brother made her insides fire up whenever he was around…well, then… "I'll just have to get over it. I can't afford to be fired from this job." Especially for the same reason she'd been let go from the last one. And that time wasn't her fault.

She left the stall and climbed up into the loft for a section of hay. As she backed down the ladder, she was just about to put her foot on the next rung when a voice sounded behind her.

"You can't sleep in the barn tonight."

Jessie spun to face the man she'd been thinking about and missed her step. She dropped the section of hay and reached out to grab hold of anything to keep herself from falling, but it was too late.

She toppled backward, bracing herself for a hard landing on her ass.

Instead, she crashed into a solid wall of muscle, and strong arms wrapped around her, pulling her close. She stared up into Brody's eyes. "Damn it, you scared me."

He shook his head, a smile tugging at the corners of his lips. "You scare too easily." He appeared tired, his eyes shadowed. "What are you doing out here after dark?"

"Checking on Scout," she said.

"In a dress?"

"Your mother's idea." She tugged at the hem in an effort to cover her thighs. In her fall, the dress had hiked up, displaying an embarrassing amount of skin.

Brody's dark eyes flared and his hands tightened around her. He appeared in no hurry to set her back on her feet, holding her weight with seemingly little effort.

"Why are you out this late?" she demanded before she could think. It was none of her business when he came and went. But with her body pressed close to his, she could barely think, much less breathe.

A shadow passed over his face. "I was working on a project and lost track of time."

"Your dinner is in the refrigerator. Why don't you go eat?"

He snorted. "I will, as soon as I make sure you don't sleep in the barn again."

Heat filled Jessie's cheeks. "That was only the first night when we were settling in. I was tired from riding all day."

"So you thought you might sleep better with your horse?"

She opened her mouth to argue and then clamped it shut. He was right. She might not have been thinking it, but she had been leaning toward bedding down in the stall again. If she was honest with herself, tonight it wasn't because she thought Scout might have a hard time adjusting to *his* new home. The truth was *she* was having a hard time adjusting to her new living arrangements.

"You can put me down," she reminded him. "I think

I'm safe from falling now." In some ways. In others, she was in grave danger with this man.

"I don't know. For as tall as you are, you're pretty lightweight."

"But I'm strong and capable of doing anything a man can." She stared straight into his eyes. Big mistake. He had the most beautiful blue eyes she could easily fall into and lose herself. "Please put me down."

"You need to be more careful coming down out of the loft." He set her on her feet and reached out to pluck a piece of straw from her hair. Then he brushed a strand of hair behind her ear, his knuckles skimming across her cheek.

Her breath caught and she fought to keep from leaning into his hand. "You need to quit sneaking up on me," she said, her voice soft and husky. Not like her usual strong, straightforward tone. What was wrong with her?

He stared at her for a long time, his hand still raised from brushing back her hair. "Anyone ever tell you that you have pretty eyes?"

She shook her head, her heart thumping hard against her ribs. Every place on her body where his hands had touched, still tingled.

Then his arm fell to his side. "If you weren't the cook, I'd…"

Jessie leaned toward him, her eyes widening. "You'd what?"

"I'd…" His gaze shifted from her eyes to her mouth and he bent closer, his lips inches from hers.

Jessie forgot when she'd taken her last breath. She

lowered her eyelids, her glance slipping to his mouth, her lips tingling. "Yes?"

For a heart-pounding, breath-stealing moment, she thought for sure he was going to kiss her.

Then Brody straightened, his brows knitting. "Nothing." He drew in a deep breath and let it out slowly. "Come with me to the house and show me where I can find my dinner."

Jessie inhaled and backed away. "There's a plate in the refrigerator. All you have to do is pop it in the microwave."

"When are you coming to the house?" he asked.

"As soon as I've fed Scout and topped off his water."

"Okay. But don't make me come out looking for you. I don't want to find you sleeping in the stall again."

"You won't," she promised, her back to him as she scooped half a bucket of feed for Scout.

The barn door opened and closed, leaving her alone at last.

Jessie pressed the bucket of sweet feed to her chest.

Holy hell. She'd almost kissed the boss. Again.

As she dropped the grain into Scout's trough, she vowed to keep her distance from the McFarlan brothers. They were entirely too attractive—especially the one whose hands on her body made her feel things she hadn't felt before, making her want so much more. But she couldn't afford for things to go wrong on this job. Scout depended on her, and she couldn't let him down.

CHAPTER SEVEN

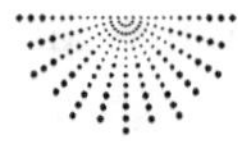

Brody woke early again the next day, dressed and carried his boots out to the kitchen.

He'd eaten slowly last night, waiting to make certain Jessie came in from the barn and went to bed in the guest bedroom. All night long, he was fully aware she was on the other side of the wall from him. He couldn't help wondering whether or not she slept in the nude. He hoped she didn't. If there should be a fire, God forbid, he wouldn't want his brothers ogling her as she stood naked in the yard.

Several times in the night, he'd been tempted to knock on her door and ask if she was all right, or if she wanted anything. The only thing keeping him from doing that was the knowledge the master suite was on the other side of the guest bedroom from him. If he knocked on the door, his mother would hear and come out to investigate. Although, as late as she'd gone to bed, she probably wouldn't be disturbed by a tornado roaring through.

His mother had gone out on a date the previous evening.

He, Angus and Colin had stayed up watching a game on television, then the news and the late shows, until their mother finally returned from her date with Carl the Heartbreaker.

She'd come in smiling. *"Why are you all still awake? It's past your normal bedtime."*

"And yours," Angus had reminded her.

She'd smiled happily. *"So it is. I'd better get to sleep. And so should you."* Their mother had gone off to bed as though coming home late were the norm, not the exception.

"I don't like it," Angus had grumbled.

"She's a grown woman," Colin had reminded him.

Brody had stared after their mother, refusing to comment—not even sure what to say if he did. He'd never thought about his mother dating.

Worry about his mother and the insistent tightness in his groin after leaving Jessie in the barn made for a crappy night's sleep. All he wanted was to avoid bumping into anyone, get to the cabin and take out his frustrations on canvas.

Unfortunately, Jessie was up and already preparing breakfast in the kitchen when he entered. The heavenly scent of frying bacon filled the air.

She hummed softly to herself, off-key and oblivious to his arrival. Wearing jeans and a faded tank top, her sleek, athletic body moved from the sink to the stove. Apparently she hadn't noticed him in the room.

Quietly he slipped his feet into his boots, hesitant to disturb the woman cooking.

Her humming stopped and she cursed when bacon grease popped out of the pan onto her hand. "Damn." She tried to reach across to turn the burner down, but more grease splattered her arm and she jerked it back.

Brody leaped to his feet and hurried across the room. He stood behind her, reached around and shifted the pan from the burner. Then he turned off the flame.

At first she jumped when his body pressed against hers. She remained stiff until he turned her around.

"Are you okay?"

"Yes," she said, staring down at her hands.

"Come with me."

He gripped her arms and walked her over to the kitchen sink. He turned on the cool water and tugged her hands beneath the spray. "Better?"

When she nodded, he turned off the water and looked down at the red dots where the grease had burned her, his thumb gently brushing over the injuries.

She didn't pull away and he didn't want to let go. All night long he'd dreamed of holding her in his arms and kissing her. Now he stood close enough he could smell the herbal scent of her shampoo and feel the warmth of her body.

When she glanced up, her gaze meeting his, her eyes widened, the gray-blue orbs darkening, her indrawn breath causing her chest to expand and her breasts to rise.

"I don't know why…" Brody gathered her closer, one hand tangling in her hair, the other sliding around to the base of her spine, tugging her against him, "…but you make me want to kiss you." He bent over her, his mouth hovering close to hers. "Tell me no and I won't." His gaze on her lips, he held his breath as she opened her mouth, he assumed to put a stop to him.

She rested her palms on his chest and could easily have pushed him away. Instead, she curled her fingers into his shirt and dragged him down to her. At the same time as she rose up on her bare feet and covered his mouth with hers, sliding her tongue across the seam of his lips.

Brody tangled his hand in the hair at the nape of her neck and deepened the kiss.

When she opened to him, he swept in and claimed her tongue, caressing, thrusting and twisting with hers in a sensual dance. He slid his other hand lower, cupping the curve of her ass, pressing her hips against his, the swell of his cock nudging her belly.

Jessie curled her hands around his neck, her breasts smashing against his chest.

"I smell bacon," a voice sounded from the back of the house.

Jessie broke away from Brody, the back of her hand rising to cover her kiss-swollen lips.

Heavy footsteps sounded on the wooden floors and Colin entered the kitchen. "Something smells good."

He stopped when he spotted Brody standing close to Jessie.

"Breakfast will…um…be in just a few minutes."

Jessie spun away from the two men and placed the pan back on the stove.

"Don't turn the heat up so high on the bacon and it won't pop like that," Brody said. "And don't set a place for me." He barely looked at Colin as he jammed his cowboy hat on his head and left through the back door.

His body on fire, his cock pushing hard against the fly of his jeans, Brody felt like he might explode. Still hungry, but for something other than food, he hopped on one of the four-wheelers he'd found in the back of the barn and headed out to the cabin.

What had he done? Jessie was an employee of the ranch. Brody was her employer. If he could square things away with his mother, and if his artwork wasn't embraced by wealthy Texans, he might not stick around. He could be back on the road to Seattle, a hell of a long way from Texas.

He didn't have room in his life for a relationship, especially with a woman who came with a horse. Not that a kiss made it mandatory to have a relationship with her, but damn. He'd thought that if he kissed her, he'd purge the desire to hold her. Boy had he been wrong. Holding Jessie in his arms, kissing her, pressing his body against hers only made him want her even more.

Coming home had become a lot more complicated than he'd anticipated.

JESSIE MANAGED NOT to burn the bacon because she didn't put it back on the burner. It'd cooked enough.

Well, almost. So it was a little droopy and not as crisp as she liked, but it wasn't burned. She'd also scrambled eggs and only burned two out of the six pieces of toast.

Angus and Colin ate everything she put before them and washed it all down with coffee.

"Don't wait dinner on me," Colin said. "I'll be late getting back today. One of my foremen is out sick and my trim guy's wife is having a baby. I'll be filling in where I can to keep things on track." He left, giving Jessie a last concerned glance.

She smiled and waved, pretending nothing was wrong or different, or that his brother hadn't kissed her so thoroughly it had rocked the world as she knew it.

"After I take care of the animals, I have to make a run into town to the hardware store if you'd like to ride along," Angus offered.

"No, thank you. If it's all right by you, I'd like to take Scout out for a ride. He could use the exercise and I'd like to see more of the Rafter M."

"You're welcome to ride anywhere on the ranch you like, as long as you close the gates behind you."

Her mouth twisted. "I grew up on a large ranch. I understand the need to keep the gates closed."

Angus nodded. "Right. I'm preaching to the choir. Be careful out riding by yourself."

"Don't worry. I've been taking care of myself for a long time." Jessie smiled at the oldest brother. "But thanks for caring."

He touched her arm. "I think you'll be a great addition to the ranch, Jessie."

"When I'm not cooking, if there's anything you need

done in the barn or anywhere, I worked with my father mending fences, castrating steers and even doing light construction repairs. I can handle a hammer like no one's business."

Angus laughed. "I believe it. I might take you up on the help later. Go for your ride and look around. A fresh perspective is always good."

Jessie cleaned the kitchen, hurriedly dragged on her boots and stuck a cowboy hat on her head. By the time she reached the barn Angus was climbing into the ranch pickup.

"I got only half the stalls clean, but I'll finish when I get back. Use whatever you need from the tack room for your ride on Scout and help yourself to feed and hay."

"Thank you." Jessie, feeling lighter and happier than she had in a long time, waited until Angus left before she turned to the work she felt more capable of.

For the next two hours, she mucked stalls and layered in fresh straw. By the time she finished, she was hot, sweaty and ready for her ride on Scout.

She took the time to check him over, clean his hooves and brush him. Then she threw a blanket on his back, and the saddle that had been her father's went on top of the blanket. Lastly, she slipped his bridle over his head.

Scout pawed the dirt, ready to get out for a run. He enjoyed going for a ride as much as Jessie did. Heading through the gate she'd seen Brody drive through the previous day, she closed it behind her and rode away from the barn and house.

Out in the open, Scout broke into a gallop, racing across pastures, over hills and down into gentle valleys. When they came to a fence, they turned and followed the fence for a while.

Jessie checked for broken wires, damaged posts and noted where they were. She could return later or another day and repair them, figuring if she made herself indispensible, the McFarlans would have to keep her on permanently.

Nearing noon, the sun beat down on her—typical Texas, hot and dry. The ground dipped into a shallow valley with a line of trees snaking the length of it, indicating a water source. Scout must have sniffed it, because he trotted down the hill and into the tree line.

A creek ran the length of the valley, the water flowing, crystal clear and inviting. Jessie dismounted and led Scout to the edge to drink.

When he'd had his fill, she looped his reins over the saddle and found a patch of grass he could munch on. She never worried about him running off. Scout was as loyal as a dog and usually stayed with her, or nearby as her protector.

The Rafter M Ranch reminded her of growing up on the Circle C in the Panhandle, when her father was foreman over eight other ranch hands. She'd had the run of the ranch from the time she was old enough to saddle her own pony. One of her favorite summer activities was swimming. The Circle C had a nice creek with a pool deep enough her feet couldn't touch the bottom in many places.

Wondering if this creek had the same, Jessie walked

upstream a few yards, pushed through a stand of willows and into an open, rocky area.

Bingo.

Nestled in the middle was a wide, deep pool, perfect for swimming.

With Angus and Colin gone from the ranch and Brody off doing whatever Brody did when he disappeared for hours, Jessie figured she had the pool all to herself. She glanced around, peered through the branches and listened. Nothing but birds singing.

She pulled her tank top over her head and draped it over a bush, then shucked her boots and jeans. Hesitating in her bra and panties, she listened again and then stripped them off as well.

With nothing but air on her skin, she walked into the water until it came up to her waist. Then she bent and pushed off, swimming across the pool, letting the clean water cool her skin and wash the dust and sweat from her body.

This was the reason she could never work in a city. She loved the land, the freedom to swim in the nude and the way she felt one with nature.

Jessie swam several laps and then flipped onto her back and floated, staring up at the sparkles of sunlight flitting through the leaves above as a gentle breeze rippled across the canopy.

With her ears in the water, sound was muffled and she felt like she was in a world all her own.

This place was magical, like a shadowy grotto, the pool surrounded by large boulders...one of which had a cowboy perched on the edge, leaning back, his gaze on her.

Jessie gasped and froze. When her arms and legs stopped moving, she sank like a rock, inhaling water as she went.

CHAPTER EIGHT

*B*rody spent the morning with his paintbrush flying over the canvas, an image emerging as he combined color and texture in bold strokes. The subject, like the day before, was the woman who'd captured his attention that morning in a kiss he wouldn't soon forget.

He hoped, by painting, to get her out of his mind. This painting turned out to be of her face as she looked up at him, her lips begging to be kissed. Rather than work her out of his system, the painting revved his libido and made him want her more.

Well past noon, he realized he hadn't moved from his position in hours, and it was getting hot.

Stretching, he decided he needed a break to work the kinks out of his shoulders and maybe head back to the house for lunch. Colin would be gone for the day. Angus might be working his horses, and his mother...

Oh hell, who knew what his mother was doing since she'd gone on strike.

Which left Jessie. Possibly alone.

He almost decided to stay and paint for the rest of the day rather than face her again. An apology was probably in order for taking advantage of her and kissing her like he did.

Brody capped his paints and moved the easel into the cabin, closing the door. He'd come back later and finish what he'd started. If only people and relationships were as easy to manage as a painting. He hadn't realized just how warm it had become until he wiped the sweat from his brow.

Instead of hopping on the four-wheeler and heading back to the ranch house, he walked over the top of the next hill and down into the valley where the old swimming hole was located. After staring at Jessie for the past several hours, he could use a cooling swim.

He'd almost reached the tree line along the creek when a movement caught his eye. A horse emerged from the brush, a saddle on his back. As Brody neared, he recognized the brindle coloring of Jessie's gelding. Fully saddled, the reins looped over the saddle horn, the horse bent to pull at a tuft of grass.

Where was Jessie?

Brody's heartbeat kicked up a notch and he lengthened his stride until he was running down the hill toward the creek. Had she been thrown? If so, was she lying facedown in the water, drowning with no one to pull her out?

Fear wrapped around Brody's heart and squeezed

his chest so hard he could barely breathe as he pushed his way through the trees and bushes and emerged onto a giant boulder overlooking the old swimming hole.

Breathing hard, his gaze swept the water, searching…

A slim, pale figure surfaced and rolled over onto her back, the water glistening on her skin.

Jessie. Naked and natural, a water nymph gliding through a sylvan pool.

She lay on her back, staring up at the canopy, a slight smile curling her lips, her arms and legs skimming the water in graceful strokes.

Brody dragged in a deep breath to calm his rampaging pulse. It did no good. Desire replaced fear, and his heart beat on in a rapid staccato. Caught in a trance, he sank down on the rock, his gaze fixed to the beauty below, his cock hardening, his body on fire, aching to take the woman into his arms and hold her, surrounded by the water, the trees and the sparkles of sunshine finding a path through the leaves above.

Even as his body lusted for her, in the back of his mind he was naturally selecting the oils it would take to capture the magic of her image on canvas. She was the muse to his art.

His brothers would laugh at his strange thoughts. But they weren't there. Brody had Jessie to himself.

She was halfway across the pool before she spotted him, her eyes widening, her arms and legs stopping their fluid motion. Then she sank beneath surface.

Brody leaped to his feet, kicked off his boots, shucked his jeans and shirt, and dove into the pool.

Jessie thrashed below the surface, apparently struggling to get her arms and legs in a position to help her.

Coming from behind her, Brody slipped his arms beneath hers and dragged her up for air.

Jessie twisted around, coughed, sputtered and clung to him as he slowly swam them to a shallower point where his feet could rest on the bottom.

Droplets streamed over her face and down her neck to her shoulders. She coughed the water from her lungs, clinging to his shoulders until she could breathe normally.

Then she stared into his face, her eyes widening again. "Holy hell, Brody!" Her glance darted to her breasts bobbing just beneath the water. "I'm naked and so are you!" With nothing to cover herself, she pressed her body against his.

He groaned at the way her skin slid over his, igniting a flame within. The coolness of the water around him did nothing to chill the rise of desire. His cock sprang to attention, bumping into her naked belly, making him even harder.

"Why are you here? Why are you holding me?" she demanded. Her fingers fluttered across his shoulders, her face tipped downward, her cheeks bright pink. "I thought I was alone."

"You went under. I was afraid you might drown." He forced himself to shrug when his entire body was tense with need.

"Let go of me."

He immediately released her and looked down as she slid into the water.

Before her head went under, she grabbed for him and pressed her body against his again. "On second thought, don't let go. You'll see me."

"Sweetheart, I saw all of you from up there on that rock."

Her brows furrowed. "You didn't have to look."

"I found your horse wandering without you in the saddle. What was I supposed to think?"

"I don't know, but you shouldn't have been sitting up there gawking at me." Jessie glanced over her shoulder. "No one was with you, I hope."

He shook his head. "I'm by myself."

He avoided putting his arms back around her waist, afraid that if he did, he wouldn't be able to let go a second time. Her body fit him perfectly and he loved the way her skin felt against his.

"So what's it to be? Are we going to stay in the water all day to spare your modesty? You didn't seem that shy when you were floating on your back, staring up at the sky."

"The sky doesn't judge." Jessie's forehead wrinkled. "Brody McFarlan, how long were you sitting there?" Her belly bumped into his rock-hard cock.

"Long enough." He reached out and gripped her around her slender waist. "You have a beautiful body."

Her hands on his shoulders tightened. "You shouldn't have looked."

"Well, I did, and I'm not at all sorry." He leaned his forehead against hers. "What are we going to do about it?"

"If you were a gentleman, you'd close your eyes while I get out of the water and dress."

"I would…" he grinned, "…if I were a gentleman."

She bit her lip. "I've never swum naked in a pool with a man."

"Seems you've been missing out." He tugged her closer. "Tell me to let go, and I will."

Jessie trembled, her nostrils flaring, her fingers digging into his shoulders. For a heart-stopping moment, she didn't say anything as she stared into his eyes. "I want you to…" Again, she bit down on her lip, her chest rising and falling on deep breaths, the tips of her nipples sliding across his skin.

"What?" he whispered, circling her back, his hands splayed low, brushing the swell of her ass. "Jessie, what do you want?"

She released the breath she'd inhaled. "I don't know. You confuse me."

Pulling the reins on his rampaging lust, he nodded. "And it's probably a good thing." As hard as he was, he had to give her the opportunity to back away. What he wanted to do and what he should do were diametrically opposed. "You work for me. I have no right to touch you."

"No. You don't." She paused, and then continued in a whisper, "Unless I give you permission." She slid her hands from his shoulders upward and linked them around his neck.

"Sweetheart, even if I weren't your boss, whatever we're feeling won't last. I might not stick around."

"What do you mean?" Her brows puckered. "You live here."

"Not for any longer than it takes to convince my mother not to sell the ranch." He still had his hands on her back. "My home is in Seattle. I'm going back."

Her hands remained on his shoulders as she slowly shook her head. "I wasn't thinking about tomorrow. And I might not be looking for commitment. I have my own life to get in order." She tugged his head down until their lips almost touched. "I don't know how to flirt or play games. I'm not a girlie girl, but since what happened in the kitchen, I find that I really want to kiss you again."

Brody groaned. "Sweet Jessie, kissing isn't all I want to do to you." He fought to hold back. "Babe, in case you haven't noticed, we're naked and your body against mine is making me all kinds of crazy."

"I'm feeling a little crazed myself." Her gaze on his lips, she threaded her fingers through his thick hair and stopped. "I'm over twenty-one, I'm on the pill and this is the first time in my life I've come close to seducing a man. If you're not interested, I'll understand."

"What part of making me crazy didn't you get?" He slipped his hands down over her ass and pulled her legs up and around his waist, his cock nudging her entrance. "And just who is seducing whom?"

"I'm seducing you." Jessie cupped his face with one hand, the other applying pressure to the back of his head. "Tell me what to do. I learn quickly."

"You're already doing it." He crushed her lips with his, giving in to the lust washing over him in a tsunami of sensations. Yet he hesitated before penetrating her. Breaking off the kiss, he whispered against her ear, "You're not a virgin, are you?"

She laughed out loud and eased down over him, taking him into her. "Not since I was sixteen in the bed of Jimmy Rae Wharton's pickup truck. I haven't been with many men since."

Brody frowned. "How many?"

She smiled. "Enough to know where things go, but not enough to wear things out."

Brody laughed and wrapped his arms around her, thrusting deep inside her.

The walls of her channel fit around him, slick and tight.

"Damn, you're tight," he said, his voice low, guttural.

"That's good, right?" Her breath caught and she closed her eyes. "Oh my."

Brody stopped before thrusting again. "Did I hurt you?"

"Yes. No." Her eyes widened, the gray-blue deepening. "Dear Lord, don't stop now." She pressed down on his shoulders, raising up and lowering herself on his staff.

Needing leverage, he backed her against the boulder and sat her on a shelf of rock beneath the water's surface. Hands free, he tucked them beneath her thighs and pumped in and out of her until she clung to him, her head thrown back, her breathing labored.

"Is this how it's supposed to feel?" she cried.

"Good or bad?" he asked.

"So good it should be bad, but it's not." She clutched

his buttocks and slammed him home. "Just don't stop, unless you want to see me all kinds of crazy."

Every nerve and blood cell raced for the finish line, while wave after wave of sensations swept over him until his body tensed, his muscles bunched and he exploded in a sparkling array of fireworks. One last thrust and he buried himself deep inside Jessie and stood still for a long, glorious moment.

When he could think with his brain again, he rested his forehead against hers. "You're amazing."

"Is it always that intense?" she whispered, her breathing ragged, her eyelids still at half-mast. "I mean, that was incredible."

"And I haven't even begun to please you."

JESSIE'S belly fluttered and her pulse leaped. "What do you mean? I *was* pleased."

"Not as much as you could be." He raised her off him and settled her higher on a rocky ledge protruding over the pool. Brody slid his hand between her knees, parting her legs.

Jessie's eyes rounded and her core burned white-hot. "What are you doing?"

His big, calloused fingers rested on her knees, a sexy smile curling the corners of his mouth. "I want to make you as crazy as you made me."

"But I *was*—"

Brody stepped between her legs and, with his tongue, flicked a path along the inside of her thigh toward her center.

Jessie's nerve endings jumped, sending an electric current zinging to her core. Jessie's breath caught on a gasp. "Oh."

Brody's chuckle sent a whisper of warm breath across her opening.

Her legs spread wider.

With his thumbs, he parted her folds.

Barely able to catch her breath, Jessie stared down at his dark head.

Brody darted his tongue out, flicking the nub of flesh.

Fire shot through her groin and outward to the tips of her fingers, her entire body trembling on the edge of…of…

He slid a thick finger into her throbbing, wet channel and flicked his tongue over her clit again.

Jessie grabbed his head in both of her hands, twisting her fingers in his hair. "Oh sweet heaven," she cried.

Another finger joined the first, stretching, massaging, pumping in and out. Brody sucked her clitoris into his mouth and flicked her, again and again.

Her cries rose above the water as the wind rippled through the trees above, the warm air wrapping around her naked body. How could it get more exquisite?

Then his tongue stroked her, swirling around that tightly packed bundle of highly agitated nerves, sending her over the top, spinning out of control.

Jessie rocketed into the stratosphere. "Brody!" she screamed, her voice echoing off the rocks and the canopy of leaves. She held on to his hair, her hips rocking with the thrusts of his tongue until her insides exploded into a million tiny fragments. Her body froze—everything, including her heart and lungs, seized for that moment.

Then the world came rushing back and she dragged in a ragged breath, her muscles going limp, her bones liquefying. Too drained to hold herself up, she sank back against the rock, her hand draping over her belly, her eyes staring vacantly at the leaves above.

Brody climbed out of the water and stretched out on the rock beside her. He leaned over her, a frown denting his forehead. "Are you okay?"

"I don't know," she said, her voice weak, her body trembling.

"Did I hurt you?"

"No." She dragged in a steadying breath. "For a moment there...I think I died." Then she turned and smiled at him, her heart filling with light and joy. "But I didn't."

Brody burst out laughing and lay back, his chest rising and falling as if he'd been running.

Jessie lay for a long time staring up at the points of light making their way through the leaves. "Thank you."

Brody didn't respond, lying still beside her. He reached for her hand and held it in his bigger one.

"Lying in the warm air, with a gentle breeze blowing through the leaves, makes you think everything is right in the world." Jessie stretched, raising her free arm over her head, her back arching off the boulder.

Brody's gaze skimmed over her body. "Isn't it?"

Her body tingled where his glance lingered. With a soft snort, Jessie answered, "For the moment."

His lips tightening, Brody said, "And then we return to reality."

Jessie sighed and gave him a sad smile. "Yes."

"Hey, why the sad face?" He touched her cheek with his fingertips. "What is it you want out of life?"

Her gaze shifted back to the leaves above and she whispered, "A home." That one word meant more to her than she'd ever realized. When her father died, she'd had no place to call home. Living with the McFarlans, she could feel the connection between the people and the ranch. She wanted that.

"You have a job, a place to live and a place for Scout," he reminded her.

"And I'm very grateful for those, but I didn't realize how important it was to have a place to call your own that no one could kick you out of, or take away from you."

Brody leaned up on his elbow and stared down at her.

His gaze made the heat rise in her cheeks. "What?" She blinked. "You don't know how it feels. I've never lived in a place that I could call my own."

"What about your parents?"

"Mom left my father when I was four. I haven't seen her since. My dad worked and lived on a big ranch in the Panhandle. We never owned the house we lived in. When my father died of a heart attack, I couldn't live there any longer. I had to move and find a place for me and Scout." She tried to pull her fingers free of his hand but he held on. "You've always had the Rafter M Ranch to come home to, even when you stayed in Seattle."

He shook his head. "Do you think a home is only a place?"

"Oh no. A home is so much more than just a place. It's where you're surrounded by the people you love, and who love you unconditionally."

Brody's gaze drifted out over the pool. "A place you feel safe and you can trust the people around you to have your back."

"Yeah." For a moment her eyes misted as she thought of her father and how happy she'd been growing up. He'd been there for her up until the day he died. Since then, she'd been homeless. "I can only work on the things I can control. I want to earn enough money to put a down payment on a place of my own, with enough acreage for Scout." She turned to Brody, reaching out to rest her hand on his chest. "Too bad you're going back to Seattle."

He stiffened. "Why?"

"I would have invited you over for dinner or a game of cards." She smiled sleepily.

His chuckle warmed her. "Would you be burning the meal?"

She tapped his chest. "I'm learning. Or maybe I'd throw a steak on the grill. I bet you don't get many sunny days in Seattle for grilling."

Brody's hand covered hers on his chest. "No, I don't. I can't remember the last time I grilled. Probably eight years ago when I lived here." He lay still for a while, his chest rising and falling beneath her hand in a steadily slowing rhythm. "Who knows, maybe I'll fly down for a visit and you can grill me that steak," he said softly.

Jessie smiled.

Though the sex had been world altering, she refused to think past this day and the sunshine making the sky so blue. No matter what tomorrow brought, nothing could take away the memory of today.

Jessie inched closer to Brody and relaxed, letting all the worry of the past couple of weeks slide off her shoulders.

The warm air and gentle breeze lulled her into a hazy, sleepy place.

Brody wrapped her in his arms and she slipped into a halo of darkness.

BRODY LAY FOR A LONG TIME, Jessie's slender body pressed against him, her leg thrown over one of his, and fought to quell the panic. He'd just made love to a woman who wore her feelings on her sleeve and, despite her argument to the contrary, would want more from him than he was ready or willing to give.

If she were just some girl he met in a bar, he'd have no trouble walking away. But Jessie was…well, Jessie. Kind, caring and generous. Hurting her would be like kicking a puppy.

Damn it, she was anything but a puppy. The woman fit him—her body just the right length, her curves complementing his hard plains. Open and sunny, she balanced his brooding, artistic nature and made him want to be better, happier.

What would happen if he didn't go back to Seattle at all? What if he stayed at the Rafter M Ranch?

He'd have to confront his eight-year-old anger at Colin, forgive him and get over the past. Hiding his work would be impossible and that meant revealing a part of him that even his family wasn't aware of—with the exception of Angus. His older brother hadn't ridiculed him or told him his work was a waste of time.

In Seattle, he'd maintained a certain anonymity while he built his portfolio. Working as a bartender at night, he'd spent the days painting. No one cared what he did or where he was from.

In Temptation, Texas, everyone knew everyone and their business. He'd wanted to prove himself before he revealed his work to those he cared the most about. He'd left, mad at his brother for betraying him. Staying away had been easier than coming home to work through his anger. To fill the lonely, empty hours of the day, he'd taken up drawing, enrolled in a class at the university and transitioned into painting.

The longer he stayed away, the harder it was to return, other than for short visits.

Now that he was here, he wasn't sure he could leave again...and he wasn't sure he could stay.

CHAPTER NINE

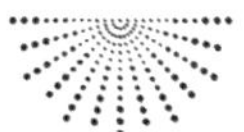

Jessie woke a little while later. The sun angling through the tree trunks, shining into her face, made her blink her eyes and glance around.

Brody lay on his back, his eyes closed, his face peaceful in sleep.

Sitting up, Jessie stared at the man who'd captured her heart in a very short time.

He was tall, ruggedly handsome, with fingers that strummed her body like a musical instrument, making it come alive in ways she'd never imagined.

Too bad he was going back to Seattle. She would love to get to know him better, to find out why he was always so brooding and angry. When he laughed, all that darkness disappeared.

Jessie wanted to be the one to make him laugh, to make his heart lighter. But she couldn't make him stay.

A gangly woman, more tomboy than girl, didn't have a chance at keeping a man like Brody McFarlan's interest.

Her chest tight, she gathered her clothing and hid in the bushes to dress and pull on her boots. Then she went in search of her horse.

Scout stood in the middle of a field, happily grazing.

When she clicked her tongue, he lifted his head, spotted her and trotted over.

With one last glance toward the stand of trees shrouding the swimming hole and the man who'd pretty much ruined her for any other, Jessie swung up into the saddle.

Ready for a run, Scout took off toward the barn, hooves flying over the dry Texas ground, kicking up dust in his wake.

Jessie leaned over the horse's neck, letting the breeze blow her hair out of her face, hoping the wind would blast the silly dreams of a happily ever after with Brody out of her mind. She'd just met him and had mad, passionate sex with the cowboy in broad daylight. It didn't mean forever. He'd been sure to say that before they got too hot and heavy into the sex.

BACK AT THE HOUSE, she quickly went to work pulling food items from the pantry and refrigerator. Mrs. McFarlan had shown her how to look up recipes on the Internet. All she had to do was follow instructions from the electronic tablet she'd left for her to use in the kitchen.

With no one interrupting her, Jessie prepared a large pot of hearty beef stew and cornbread.

At the end of the day, Angus and Colin returned to the smell of a tasty dinner. The stew simmered on the stove and a tub of butter and honey sat on the table.

Mrs. McFarlan arrived home from town in time to join them.

Jessie sat with the family, barely touching her food, quietly acknowledging the compliments without really engaging. Her attention focused on the sounds outside, hoping Brody would come back to the house and join the rest of the family for dinner. Her body hummed, her pussy still throbbing from Brody's thorough lovemaking.

He didn't return to the house until after dark.

THE NEXT DAY was much like the previous. Jessie and Brody settled into a routine of avoidance. When they did run into each other, the electricity in the air sizzled. But Brody refused to act on it, and Jessie wasn't going to be the one to initiate contact this time.

Perhaps it was better this way. If Brody was leaving, they shouldn't take whatever was between them any farther.

No matter what she told herself, Jessie couldn't deny the heat burning beneath the surface, nor could she turn it off like a burner on the stove.

BY FRIDAY, her nerves were so frayed she dropped pots

and pans in the kitchen, burned the toast and would have ruined their dinner if Mrs. McFarlan hadn't come into the kitchen in time to stop her from torching the pan of fried chicken.

Mrs. M turned off the flame and faced Jessie. "Honey, what's wrong? You're wound up tighter than a rattlesnake with a new button."

Jessie wrung her hands, tears filling her eyes. She couldn't tell Mrs. M that the cook had foolishly fallen for the boss. "Nothing. I'm fine."

"You're not fine." The older woman studied her, her eyes narrowing. Finally, she said, "What you need is to get out of the house, have a little fun. You're young. You should be dating, seeing other people. Making friends."

Jessie shook her head. "I can't afford to go out. I have to earn my keep."

"Oh nonsense. Wear a dress. The men will buy your drinks and ask you to dance. You won't need a dime with a figure like that."

"I can't do that. I've always paid my own way."

"Oh, sweetheart, you have to have more confidence in yourself." Mrs. M held her at arm's length and stood back, her gaze sweeping Jessie's length. "You're a pretty girl. Isn't she, Colin?" She glanced up.

Jessie looked over her shoulder.

Colin had entered the room, a grin spreading across his face. "Who, Jessie?"

Mrs. M frowned. "Yes, Jessie."

Colin tilted his head to the side. "Sure, she's pretty."

"Any man would love to date her," Mrs. M insisted.

"Sure. Sure." Colin looked over their shoulders. "What's for supper?"

Mrs. McFarlan wound up a dish towel and popped Colin's ass with it. "You're hopeless."

"What?" He rubbed his back pocket. "I didn't get any lunch. I'm starving."

"You should take Jessie to the Ugly Stick Saloon tonight and introduce her around. She hasn't been out since she got here."

"She met everyone last week. That's where we found her."

Mrs. M planted her fist on her hip. "It's Friday night. Are you going out?"

Colin frowned. "Maybe."

"Good. You're taking Jessie." The older woman scowled at Colin. "No wonder you boys aren't married yet. You're completely clueless!" She shooed him out of the kitchen. "Dinner won't be ready for another thirty minutes. Out of here!"

Colin shrugged and grinned at Jessie. "We can see if Angus wants to join us as designated driver. It's been a tough week. I could stand a beer or two." He winked and left the room.

"Mrs. McFarlan, I can't go with Colin."

"Why not?" The older woman turned the burner on and set the flame lower than it had been before. "You didn't already have a date, did you?"

"No, but you practically forced Colin to take me out tonight." Jessie bit her lip. "I don't want to be a pity date. Besides, he might have another girl in mind, and I would be in the way."

"Then go as friends. That way you aren't with anyone and you can flirt with all the men." She shook her head. "Jessie, I've been out of the dating scene for decades, and I know more about it than you and my sons. Sheesh. Amateurs." She grinned to soften her words. "Go. I like you and want you to be happy."

Jessie wasn't going to talk the woman out of her plan and she didn't want to disappoint her, so she agreed.

Mrs. McFarlan helped her through the batch of fried chicken and beat the lumps out of the mashed potatoes before the men returned to the kitchen, showered and dressed in clean jeans and shirts.

As usual, Brody hadn't arrived at the house by the time the rest of the family sat down to eat. Jessie joined them and laughed and talked with Angus and Colin, learning more about Colin's challenges as a construction contractor, from frame carpenters who didn't show up for the job to lazy bricklayers.

Angus glanced across the table at Colin. "By the way, thanks for finishing up mucking the stalls again."

Jessie's cheeks heated, but she didn't dispute Angus's assumption.

"I don't know what you're talking about." Colin bit into a juicy chicken leg and chewed.

"If you haven't been clean the stalls this week, has Brody?" Angus asked

Colin shook his head. "Brody hasn't been around the house or barn all week. As soon as the sun rises, he's gone."

Mrs. M stared across at Jessie. "Jessie, did you muck the stalls?"

Her cheeks burning, Jessie nodded.

"You're the cook, Jessie." Angus's brows drew together. "You don't have to work in the barn too. Though we appreciate all you do."

"I like working outside," she insisted. "I've done it all my life."

"Dinner was delicious." Colin stared down at the bone in his hand. "Is there anything you can't do?"

"Maybe you should take Jessie with you on the job," Angus suggested. "She's been a big help with the horses this week. She knows as much as I do, if not more, about hoof disease and the best feeds to buy. I'll bet she could run circles around your frame carpenters. She helped me fix the boards on the corral fence. She can swing a hammer."

"What, and not smash her thumb, like you?" Colin nodded at the bandage on Angus's thumb.

Angus grinned sheepishly. "Yeah, well, she is good at it."

Colin stared at Jessie, his eyes narrowing, assessing her. "Have you ever framed anything?"

"I helped my dad build a pole barn, a chicken coop and a toolshed. I know one end of the hammer from the other."

Angus laughed. "See? There isn't anything she can't do."

"Even cooking." Colin grinned.

Her cheeks continued to burn from all the attention. "Normally I'm hopeless at the usual girl things. My father had me doing ranch maintenance work from as early as I can remember."

"What kind of girl things do you not know how to do?"

She shook her head, her face so hot she thought it would explode. "Never mind."

"No, really." Colin leaned forward. "What do you not know?"

"I'm really okay with the way I am."

"Come on, Jessie, you wouldn't have brought it up if you didn't want to know. Angus and I might be able to help you, as long as it isn't putting on makeup and fixing hair."

"I've got that covered," Mrs. McFarlan said. "But I'm interested to hear how you're going to teach our Jessie about girl things." She leaned back, her lips curling into a mischievous grin. "Go on, Jessie. What else would you like to know?"

Jessie lifted a shoulder and let it fall. "I don't know. Flirting has always escaped me."

"That's easy." Colin laughed. "Just watch."

He turned to Angus and made a big show of batting his eyes. "Angus, honey," he said in a falsetto voice, "you're so big and strong. I could use a man like you to protect me."

Angus's brows knit. "She could wipe the floor with you. Why would Jessie need a man to protect her?"

Jessie laughed. "Exactly."

Colin sighed. "You have to stroke a man's ego. They all think they're big and tough and their girl is small and defenseless."

Mrs. McFarlan shook her head. "No wonder you don't have a girlfriend, Colin. Women are stronger than you think. They want someone who is their equal to share their lives with. All the flirting and pretending to be someone you aren't is exhausting."

"That's all I've got." Colin turned to Angus. "Your turn."

Jessie raised her hand. "That's okay. I'll just be me, if it's all the same to you."

Angus shrugged. "I like you just the way you are."

"So do I," Mrs. McFarlan said.

"I was only trying to help," Colin insisted. "I like Jessie just the way she is too."

Footsteps sounded and Brody appeared, his broad shoulders filling the doorway. His gaze swept the people at the table and stopped at her, his blue eyes darkening.

Jessie's pulse leaped and butterflies stormed her belly.

"Brody, you're in time to settle this," Mrs. McFarlan said.

"Settle what?" He removed his hat and hung it on a peg on the wall.

"Should Jessie work at being more girlie by learning how to flirt, or stay the way she is?"

Brody's gaze never left Jessie's. "Why is this important?"

"What if she wants to date? Do you men expect a woman to flirt and fawn all over you? Or would you prefer her to be natural and straightforward?"

A frown pulled his brows low. "Jessie's fine the way she is." Brody seemed to tear his gaze away from her and turned to his mother. "Could we talk?"

The older McFarlan nodded. "Of course. What is it you want to talk about?"

He glanced at his brothers. "Alone."

Her smile faded. "Of course." Mrs. McFarlan pushed her chair back from the table and stood. "Want to take it into the office?"

"Yes, ma'am." He walked across the kitchen and stood in the hallway.

Mrs. McFarlan nodded as she passed Angus and Colin, hooked Brody's arm and led him away. "Have a good time, Jessie."

Brody glanced over his shoulder, his gaze meeting Jessie's. Then he was gone.

Jessie let go of the breath she'd been holding the entire time Brody was in the kitchen. Why couldn't she forget what happened days ago and get on with her life? Apparently, Brody had put it behind him. He certainly didn't want a repeat performance.

Well, to hell with him. "Stack your dishes in the sink when you're done eating. I'll wash them later. I'll be ready to go in five minutes." If she could figure out how to apply mascara without gouging her eyes.

As she walked by the closed door of the office, she strained to hear the rumblings behind the thick wooden door. What had Brody wanted to talk to his mother about? Was he telling her he would be leaving soon to return to Seattle?

Despite her decision to go, Jessie figured it would be a push to have a good time when she'd be thinking about Brody leaving. What she really wanted to do was storm into the office and demand he look at her and tell her he didn't feel something special the other day. That he didn't want to do it again and again.

But she was afraid he didn't feel the same. One time with her had been enough for him…and not nearly enough for her.

TWENTY MINUTES LATER, Brody walked out of the office, no further along than when he'd walked in. No manner of argument would budge his mother. She was determined to see her boys happily married and living in Texas.

Brody knew if he remained in Texas any longer, he might do something stupid like stay. The week had been long and painful. Every time he saw Jessie, he wanted to hold her so badly he ached with the need. How he'd managed to steer clear, he wasn't certain. By Friday, he'd been past caring and ready to move on or go insane. He wasn't the right man for Jessie.

She deserved a man who wasn't still trying to find himself or determine where he fit in the world. His argument with Colin had long since ceased being the reason he stayed away from Texas. He didn't know what he wanted. He didn't have any lasting feelings for Fancy Wilson and he couldn't care less if Colin slept with her again. Fancy held back too much of herself. He'd never really known where he stood with her, nor felt like sharing his deepest secrets and dreams with her.

In Seattle, he'd just started making a living from his artwork. A darned good living. If he moved from Seattle, where he'd built a following and a name for himself, he might have to start over. The people in Texas might have different taste.

Then again, he could work the ranch and make his living off cattle sales. If they met his mother's demands, he could live there with his brothers and build a house of his own. Make it his home, surrounded by family, with all their children growing up together. He didn't need his art to pay off.

If only the decision were that simple. If only it were not tied to his brothers' desires to please their mother.

Jessie knew what she wanted and she'd get it, with or without a man in her life. Jessie's goals, like everything else about Jessie, were clear and uncomplicated.

"Brody, if you want to go back to Seattle...go." His mother had told him what he'd wanted to hear.

Then she'd stuck it to him. *"But if you do, I will sell the ranch. I'm tired of holding on to something my husband loved but my boys couldn't care less about. I certainly don't need it. I could get on with my life much easier without it."*

"Where would Angus go? He's got his horse breeding program off the ground and doing great."

"He'll manage. It hasn't been fair of me to hold on to him for so long. He needs to get on with his life too."

"He stayed because he loves this place and *you."*

"And you don't?"

"The Rafter M Ranch is a part of me. Whether I live here or not, my memories will go with me."

"And what about your family?" His mother had straightened her back, her chin held high, a glassy sheen in her eyes. *"Don't you love us?"*

"Oh, Mom. You know I love you and I'm sorry I haven't been around as much as you'd like."

"I know you have to live your own life, but why can't you live it closer to home? I want to see you happy, with a family of your own, and grandkids for me to spoil."

"What if those aren't things I want?"

"Isn't there anyone you've met in the last eight years you've been close to? Someone you could see yourself sharing your life with? The good times and the bad?"

If she'd asked him that question two weeks ago, he'd have easily answered with a firm no. Not one woman he'd met along the way, including his ex-fiancée, made him want to share his life. An image of Jessie floating in the swimming hole, her body a pale, shimmering silhouette, came to mind. Another of her lying beside him on the boulder, staring up at the leaves, followed close behind.

"Was there one?" his mother had prodded, her eyes wide, hopeful.

He'd shaken himself out of the trance. *"No. But, Mom, you can't sell the ranch."*

Her lips had firmed. *"It's mine. Your father left it to me. I can and will sell it if my sons don't care enough about it to do as I asked."*

"That's blackmail."

"I don't care what you call it." She'd crossed her arms. *"They're my terms and they stand."*

"But Angus has a girlfriend and they're serious. He wants to ask her to marry him. He's waiting to see what will happen with the ranch."

She'd raised her brows. *"I guess you and Colin better get busy then."*

Angry and frustrated, Brody left the office and walked out onto the front porch in time to see Colin drive off with Jessie in the front seat of his truck.

"What the hell?"

At the same time, a call came through on his cell phone, the device vibrating in his back pocket. He jerked it out and hit the Answer button without looking at the Caller ID, thinking maybe it was Jessie telling him she'd be right back.

It was his agent, Sharon Gise. "Brody, I have good news, but we have to act fast."

"What news?" His gaze on the disappearing truck, Brody was only half listening.

"I got you into a prestigious art exhibit in downtown Dallas. They had an artist drop out at the last minute. It's next weekend. I emailed photos of your Seattle paintings and they loved them, but because it's Dallas, they'd like to know if you have anything with Texas landscapes. Please tell me you've been working while you've been home."

"I have."

"Fabulous. I can crate what you have in the gallery up here and have it there in three days. I'll need you to send photos of what you've done since, so I can go through them and forward what I think they want. How soon can you send the photos?"

"Is an hour soon enough?" Brody asked, wondering where the excitement for his craft had gone. This was his chance to go big in Texas, and all he could think about was Colin taking off with *his* girl. Again.

"The sooner the better. The gallery director is scrambling and on call for whatever you can deliver." Sharon paused and added, "The people going to this exhibit are the rich and famous of Dallas. You'll need to be there."

Her words broke through his fog of anger and he focused on Sharon for the moment. "What do you mean, I need to be there?"

"They want to meet the artist."

"You know I don't like to go to these things," he said.

"If you want to get into this gallery, you have to be present for the opening of the exhibit. Two hours, tops. Don't say no. Take the pictures and think about it. It's a chance to break out of the Seattle market and let others see what a talented artist you are."

"I'll get you those photos. But no promises."

"Hurry."

He ended the call.

"Was that your boss?" his mother's voice said from behind him.

Brody turned. "Sort of."

"Does he want you back in Seattle?" His mother's face looked so sad it pained him to hurt her so much. Despite her threats, she was his mother and the only parent he had left. Which was still more than Jessie had.

"No, actually. She wants me in Dallas," he said.

His mother's face brightened.

He raised his hand. "Don't get your hopes up. It's a one-time deal."

Her face fell like a flower drooping from lack of water. "You can't blame a mother for hoping." She looped her purse over her shoulder and stepped around him. "I'm going out. Don't wait up for me. I might be late."

Brody frowned. "Where are you going?"

She smiled. "To play cards with friends. You should get out tonight. I don't know where you've been all week, but you need to lighten up. Go dancing or something."

Brody stared at the road leading away from the ranch. The dust had already settled from where Colin's truck had gone. "Where was Colin headed?"

"He and Jessie went to the Ugly Stick Saloon. You should go." She pecked him on the cheek. "I love you, Brody. Whatever you do, have a good time."

Then she stepped down from the porch, climbed into her SUV and drove away, leaving Brody alone at the house.

For a few seconds longer he watched his mother's vehicle and then he spun around and headed for his bedroom. He grabbed his camera and hurried out to his truck. If he hurried, he could take the photos, send them to his agent and still make it to the Ugly Stick Saloon before the night got going.

With his camera on the front seat of his pickup, Brody drove out to the hunting cabin.

Twenty minutes later he had the photos he needed and returned to the house to download them to his laptop. He sent them to Sharon along with his decision about attending the exhibit.

As soon as he hit the Send key, Brody raced through a shower and shave, and dressed in his best blue jeans, boots and crisp white shirt. He was headed to the Ugly Stick Saloon without a clear plan in mind. All he knew was Jessie would be there, and he couldn't stay away another moment.

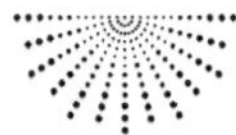

CHAPTER TEN

Audrey greeted Jessie like an old friend, hugging her as close as she could get with her pregnant belly in the way. "I'm so glad things are working out with you and the McFarlans. I'm sure they can't live without you by now."

Jessie forced a smile she didn't feel. Audrey had enough on her mind. She didn't need Jessie's pathetic problems to weigh her down any more than she already was, with a bar to run, a baby on the way and a gorgeous man waiting on her hand and foot. Yeah, Audrey was a lucky woman. She had it all.

Until she met Brody, Jessie had been satisfied to be just Jessie. Now that she'd had a taste of what it could be like to be with a man she cared about, she knew what she was missing and it hurt like a physical ache, wrenching at her gut.

"Hey, you're supposed to be having a good time."

Colin slid onto the barstool beside her. "We've been here an hour and you haven't danced once."

She glanced out at the dance floor, with no desire to get out there when all she could think about was Brody.

A cowboy stepped in front of her and held out his hand. "Wanna dance?"

Jessie gave him a weak smile and shook her head.

Colin snorted. "And not from the lack of men asking."

Glancing down at the short, creamy-white dress made of layers of silk and sheer fabric that Mrs. McFarlan insisted made her look like a sassy angel, Jessie felt like a fraud. The dress was made for a woman who should be the life of any party. That wasn't Jessie.

"You're hot, Jessie. You should be dancin', not sitting here moping. Is it something I said?"

She smiled halfheartedly. "No, Colin. You've been more than generous with your time. You should be out there dancing with all the pretty girls."

His gaze slipped to one woman nursing a beer at the other end of the bar.

Jessie's eyes narrowed. "Isn't that Fancy Wilson?"

He looked away. "Who?"

She knew darned well he'd seen the woman. He'd glanced that way more than once while he was talking to Jessie. "Why don't you ask Fancy to dance?"

"Nah. If she wanted to dance, she'd at least look up."

"Maybe she's waiting for someone to ask her." Jessie rolled her eyes. "Your mother is right. I don't know how to flirt, but you can be clueless. I swear I've seen her looking this way as many times as you've looked toward her."

"Yeah, what you don't understand is that she's off-limits."

"What?" Jessie stared at him. "I don't see any signs posted."

"She won't dance with me, go out with me or engage in anything other than the polite conversation of a stranger with me."

"What did you do to her?"

He stared down at the dregs in the bottom of his mug of beer. "I made love to her when she was engaged to my brother."

Jessie digested that admission, pieces of the puzzle coming together. "Wow. I can see why he was angry."

Colin slumped on his barstool, wrapping his hand around his mug. "I don't blame him."

"But, Colin, that was eight years ago."

"I lost the girl I love, and my brother, because of one night."

Jessie glanced over at Fancy at the same time the woman looked her way.

The pain in the other woman's eyes was evident before she looked away, color rising in her cheeks.

Colin glanced at Fancy again.

"Are you in love with her?" Jessie asked.

Colin's gaze returned to his empty mug. "Wouldn't matter if I was. She won't have anything to do with me. And I won't betray my brother again."

Jessie thought *her* life was complicated—she was in love with Brody, but he didn't love her.

If Brody still loved Fancy and Colin loved her too… someone was going to get hurt all over again.

No wonder Brody didn't want to stay in Texas or make love to Jessie more than once. He still had feelings for Fancy. Hell, he might have been thinking of Fancy when he made love to her in the swimming hole. And *she'd* seduced him. What an idiot she was.

Her head spinning and her heart breaking, Jessie couldn't sit there and do nothing. "Colin, I'd like to dance now."

"Huh?" He looked up confused.

Jessie grabbed his hand and dragged him off his stool. "If you're not going after her, you might as well dance with me. It beats mooning over someone you can't have." Her eyes stung as she led him out onto the dance floor, determined to take her own advice.

Colin stopped on the sideline, shaking his head. "Jessie, I just don't feel like dancing now."

"You don't have a choice. My father always said it was rude of a man to refuse to dance when a girl asked him." She smiled up at him. "And he taught me how to dance, so do my father proud and dance with me."

The lively tune that had been playing ended, and the band segued into a slower, haunting melody.

Colin took her hand. "If we're going to do this, let's do it like we mean it. Did your daddy teach you to waltz?"

"Yes, he did." Jessie stepped into Colin's arms. "He told me he'd fallen in love with my mother during a waltz." She smiled up at him. "Don't worry. I don't expect you to fall in love with me the same way. Just dance."

After they'd made one complete circle around the floor, her senses came alive. She knew Brody had entered the saloon, even before she spotted him standing at the edge of the dance floor.

His gaze latched on to her and Colin, his blue eyes dark, his brows dipped low.

"Why is Brody glaring at me?" Colin spun Jessie around to get a better look at his brother. "You'd think I stole his fiancée all over again."

Jessie kept her eyes forward, refusing to swivel her head to see Brody.

Colin turned Jessie under his arm. For a brief moment, she caught a glimpse of Brody's brooding face and her heart thrilled. "Oh, he does look mad."

For a giddy second Jessie dared to think Brody might be jealous of his brother Colin. Then she remembered Colin had slept with his fiancée. Maybe Brody wasn't so much jealous as angry that Colin might be trying to take another woman he'd shown even the slightest interest toward. Perhaps his anger was more about his distrust of his brother than his desire for her.

A surge of annoyance charged through Jessie's system, stiffening her spine and making her want to show Brody what he was missing by pushing her away. She'd also prove to him that she could get on with her life, whereas he still insisted on living in the past.

She grinned up at Colin. As they passed close to Brody, she threw him a vague smile and returned her gaze to Colin. Colin waltzed to the other end of the floor, going with the flow of the other dancers.

When they circled back around, Fancy Wilson stood beside Brody, her hand on his shoulder, leaning close enough to touch his ear with her lips.

A sharp pain stabbed through Jessie's heart and she stumbled.

Colin pulled her close to keep her from falling. When he glanced up, he stiffened. "Damn." His lips pressed together and he slowed, turning her around again.

Brody took Fancy in his arms and whirled her onto the dance floor, bearing down on Colin and Jessie.

Before Jessie could move away, the two stopped and faced them.

"Care to trade?" Brody asked.

Without waiting for Colin's permission, he took Jessie's hand and pulled her into his arms, clamping her tightly against him.

The music drifted into another slow song, but Jessie's heart didn't relax at all, now that she was pressed against Brody.

"Why did you butt into our dance?" she demanded, her voice not nearly as forceful as she'd intended.

"Why are you here with Colin? Did he ask you out on a date?"

Jessie snorted. "So suddenly you care? Based on the fact you avoided me all week, I assumed you weren't interested." She stopped in the middle of the music and stepped away. "If you'll excuse me, I don't want to dance with you."

He didn't release her hand, tugging her back around to face him. "I thought we had something."

"Did we?" She raised her eyebrows. "It must have been all that fresh Texas air that made you dizzy. I remember you saying something about you were leaving as soon as you could."

Brody's hand tightened around hers, his lips thinning.

Jessie shifted her glance to his hand, and fought the burn of tears building in her eyes. This wasn't how she imagined Brody coming back to her. "Leave me alone, Brody," she said softly, her throat closing on a sob. "I know how to be on my own. You know too. It's easy to insulate yourself from being hurt when you don't have anyone else in your life." She shook loose from his hand and darted through the other couples still dancing.

Jessie didn't look back. It wouldn't have done any good. She couldn't have seen anything more than the blur of tears obstructing her vision. Headed for the bar, she hoped to slip out the back door before Brody caught up to her, if he even bothered to follow.

Running past the end of the bar, Jessie was glad to see Greta Sue, the bouncer, wasn't standing guard over the hallway leading to the rear exit, giving her a clear shot at escape. Once she got outside, she wasn't sure what she'd do, but she wouldn't have to face Brody with tears in her eyes.

Audrey and Jackson emerged from the storeroom, straightening their clothes, happy, but appearing a little guilty. Her dress hitched high on the swell of her belly.

Audrey spied Jessie and stepped in front of her.

"What's wrong?" she demanded. "Did one of the rednecks make a pass at you? Point at him, and I'll rip him a new asshole."

"No. No. I'm okay, I just need some air."

"Isn't that Brody McFarlan headed our way?" Audrey asked, rubbing a hand over her belly.

Jessie shot a glance over her shoulder and her heart sped. She gripped Audrey's arms. "Do you mind if I let myself out the back door?"

"Not at all, but don't you want to wait and find out why Brody is waving at us?" Audrey nodded toward the man.

"No. I'm feeling really awful." And heartbroken.

"Then, by all means, go." Audrey eyed Brody, who was slowed down by three drunken cowgirls flinging themselves in front of him.

As Jessie passed Jackson, the big Kiowa cowboy, he put out his hand. "You sure you're running from Brody? Or are you running from yourself?" he asked, his gaze pinning her, seeming to see straight through to her heart.

The tears welled up and spilled over. "I don't want him to see me cry," she said.

"Jackson, sweetie, let her go. You men like to think women are weak. We don't like to give you proof." Audrey winked at Jessie. "Do you have a ride home?"

Jessie pressed a hand to her mouth and shook her head. "No."

Audrey nodded to Jackson. "Show her to the storeroom while I round up one of your brothers to take her home."

Jackson hooked her arm and led her to the door from which he and Audrey had just emerged. "You can hide in here while Audrey finds someone to take you home."

"What if Brody sees me going in?" she asked.

"I'll do what I can to run interference."

Her lips trembled as she touched the big Kiowa's arm. "Thank you."

Jackson held the door open for her and pulled it closed behind her.

The small storeroom was filled from floor to ceiling with boxes of liquor, cases of beer and other items the bar sold. Jessie listened at the door for the sound of footsteps but could hear nothing but the low thumping of the bass guitar. If Brody did follow her, he might stick his head in the door and see her standing there like a scared child who'd rather hide than face the truth —he didn't love her.

Jessie walked around a stack of boxes filling the center of the room, sat on several labeled *Jack Daniel's Whiskey* and waited out of sight of the door.

How long did it take to find Jackson's brothers?

She worried her bottom lip and stared around the room. A small riding crop hung from a hook on the wall.

Jessie frowned. What was a riding crop doing hanging in a storeroom?

On another hook hung a pair of bright-red leather chaps, too small for a man, but just right for a woman. Again, why would Audrey keep chaps in the storeroom when she had a costume room backstage? Jessie had seen it the night she'd grilled burgers at the saloon.

The door opened, and the music swelled, filling the room. Jessie's heart leaped and she stood, carefully peering around the boxes.

"Just a case of Miller Lite? What about Coors?" Charli Sutton shouted from the door of the storeroom over the sound of the band. She lifted a case of Miller Lite and left.

Jessie sank back onto the box as the door swung closed and shut with a click. For a brief moment she'd thought Brody followed her into the storeroom. That desperate part of her searching for love wished it had been him. Alas, it had been Charli, Audrey's cute, little, blond-haired assistant manager, with more spunk in her little pinky than most women had in their entire bodies.

With a sigh, Jessie debated pulling one of the bottles out of a box and downing it to gain a little liquid courage, enough to face Brody and pretend it didn't matter if he was going back to Seattle.

But it would be a big, fat lie. It mattered. A lot. Tears sprang to her eyes all over again. What was wrong with her? Her daddy brought her up to take the hard knocks on the chin and never let anyone see her cry. She was tougher than that.

She sniffed. Apparently not.

"Jessie, baby, why are you crying?" A deep, warm voice whispered next to her.

She jumped at the sound, tripped over a case of

Guinness and would have fallen if big hands hadn't reached out and grabbed her around the waist.

Brody yanked her into his arms and held her until she regained her balance.

When she laid her palms against his chest to push away, he wouldn't loosen his hold.

"Let go of me," she said, her voice hitching on a sob.

"Not until you tell me why you ran away from me." He touched a finger to her cheek, capturing a tear. "And why you're crying."

She shook her head, her heart hurting so badly and anger building the longer he held her and refused to let go. She slapped her palms against his chest and left them there. "You."

"What about me? Have I done something to make you afraid of me? Something that would make you run away?"

"No. I just don't want to be near you." Being with him made her soul ache and reminded her of what she didn't have. Someone to love, and to be loved by. She was alone in the world and had the misfortune to fall for a guy who wanted nothing more than a one-night stand.

"Jessie." He tipped her head up. "Why?"

"You and I don't want the same things out of life. Why should I be with you? Why did you come after me? Just stay away from me, like you have all week."

He nodded, brushing his thumb over her cheek. "I should stay away from you. And I tried."

Her throat constricted on the next sob rising up. She was right. He *had* been avoiding her. "Well, don't worry.

I won't bother you. I know when I'm not wanted. And you never promised anything beyond what happened." She reached up to pull his hand away from her face.

"Listen, Jessie."

"No. I'm done listening. I just want to be left alone." Tears spilled down her cheeks and she muttered, "Damn. Now see what you've done? I don't cry in front of people. I didn't want to cry in front of you, your ex-fiancée or any of the McFarlans. I'm tougher than that. My daddy didn't raise a sissy girl."

His chuckle sent a new wave of anger through her.

But then he brushed his lips over her forehead. "Jessie, do you ever shut up?"

"No. I don't want to hear what you have to say. Just go away and—"

Brody's lips covered hers, cutting off the run-on diatribe she'd started.

Having grown up thinking she was strong and could handle anything, Jessie now realized she was weak and emotional, like any other girl, and it made losing Brody even harder.

"Damn you," she said against his lips, her arms wrapping around his neck, pulling him closer. "Damn you." And she kissed him with all the pent-up frustration she'd collected over the week she'd avoided him as much as he'd avoided her.

Their tongues met in a wild tangle of thrusts and caresses, rough but gentle, teasing and passionate.

Brody slid his hands down her back and up under her dress.

Jessie yanked the buttons loose on his shirt and ran

her hands across his naked chest, reveling in the solid planes and rippling muscles. What she wouldn't give to be back at the creek, naked and staring up at the stars through the blanket of leaves.

When Brody's thumbs skimmed up her sides and brushed beneath her breasts, she drew in a deep breath, arching her back, pressing closer to his hands.

He dropped them to the hem of her dress and dragged it up her torso and over her head, draping it on a shelf beside her.

Jessie reached up behind her and released the hooks on her bra.

Brody slid the straps down her arms. "Aren't you afraid someone will walk in?"

"I don't care." She was with Brody. He'd come for *her*, not Fancy. That's all that mattered. "No one will see us back here." Leaning forward, she tongued a hard brown nipple, her fingers tugging the button loose on his jeans. "Are you afraid?" She slid the zipper down, and his cock sprang free, into her palms.

His breath hissed in. "No."

She glanced up at him, her hand wrapping around him. "Look. I know the deal. Live in the moment, expect nothing from tomorrow. So what are you waiting for?"

He dragged in a breath, his body stiff and his cock rock-hard. "That's not why I came in here. I wanted to tell you—"

"And I told you I didn't want to listen." She released him, backed up and slipped her panties over her hips. "Do you want me?" she said, baring herself to him, praying for one last chance at holding him close.

"Damn, Jessie." He stepped forward, wrapped his hands around her waist and lowered them over her buttocks to cup the backs of her thighs. Then he lifted her onto a stack of boxes. "I want you more than I can begin to tell you."

"Then shut up and show me." Jessie grabbed his hand, drawing him closer.

"We don't have to do this. We should talk."

"If you start talking, I'll dress and walk out of this storeroom. It's your choice."

Her hand closed around his length, sliding low to cup him. She had one chance to show him how she felt, and she'd make this time the best. It might be the last.

"Do you want to stop?" she challenged, massaging his balls between her fingers.

He closed his eyes, and heaved a sigh. "We really need to talk." His dick surged against her hand and he opened his eyes. "But no. I don't want to stop."

She guided him to her.

He halted, poised at her opening, and then backed away. "Not yet."

Brody reached for the riding crop.

Her pulse galloping, Jessie's core tightened. "What are you going to do with that?"

With the tip of the leather instrument, he tapped the inside of her thighs, urging her to spread her legs wider.

She did, her chest rising and falling with rapid breaths. Her nerves tingled where the crop rested against the inside of her knee and cream dribbled from her channel as he slid the leather tip toward her center.

Jessie cupped one of her breasts and squeezed. The

closer he moved, her legs widened as if on their own. When he reached the lips of her entrance, he raised the crop and brushed it over her curly mound. "Do you like that?"

"It's…" she drew in a ragged breath and let it go on a breathy laugh, "…inspiring."

Brody stepped between her legs and dragged the crop over the mounds of her breasts and down between them, over her belly, angling toward the apex of her thighs.

She gave a strangled chuckle. "And I wondered why someone hung a riding crop and chaps in the storeroom."

"Audrey and Jackson have been known to make love in here. I hear this is where their baby was conceived."

Brody bent forward and sucked one of Jessie's nipples into his mouth. He tapped the tip and rolled it on his tongue before moving to the next one, catching it between his teeth.

Jessie's core heated, her body humming with desire. She wanted him inside her, but she also didn't want him to stop what he was doing with his tongue. Her fingers dug into his thick hair and held him close as she arched her back, urging him to take more.

He did, sucking her breast deep into his mouth, laving the nipple into a hard little point. Then he slipped down her torso, dropping to one knee as he went.

Her heart thundering against her ribs, Jessie held her breath as he closed in on the mound of curls over her sex. He was going there. Like he had the day at the pool when he'd licked her and tongued that special place that set her world on fire.

Brody parted her folds with the rough tips of his fingers and the riding crop, sending electric currents zinging through her body, like fireworks on the Fourth of July.

As he swept his tongue across her clit, Jessie rocked her hips forward, offering him everything She was powerless to hold back, to tell him to stop what he was doing. The saloon could burn down around her, and she wouldn't care. What he was doing made her forget everything, including why she'd gone into the storeroom to begin with.

Brody swirled his tongue around the bundle of nerves, relentless in his attack, conquering her with his moves, his fingers sliding into her, one then two and three, pumping in and out of her wet channel.

The tension increased until she flung back her head, her body stiff, the maelstrom of sensations ricocheting off her insides. She catapulted over the edge, her core pulsating, thrumming fast to the galloping beat of her heart.

She dragged Brody up by his ears. "I want you inside me. Now."

He stood, positioned himself at her entrance and then thrust his cock into her, driving deep until he'd fully sheathed himself. Moving in and out, he increased his speed, with each thrust rocking the stack of boxes with the force of his desire.

Holding on, Jessie's breath caught and held, teetering on the brink of another burst of orgasmic fireworks.

Friction heated her core, setting her insides ablaze. Tingling began at her center and rippled outward in waves, ricocheting from nerve to nerve. She cried out and dug her nails into Brody's shoulders.

He thrust one last time and held her hips tight against him, burying himself inside her for a shuddering release.

Jessie wrapped her legs around him, pressing her heels into his buttocks, clamping him as close as she could, her arms around his middle, her face pressed to his chest. If it were possible to freeze that moment in time, she would have. Making love to Brody could not have been more perfect.

The squeak of a door hinge and the rush of music into the room marked the end of what just occurred.

"Jessie?" Audrey called out. She stepped around the stack of boxes and stopped, pressing a hand to her belly. "I'm so sorry to interrupt. But I found you a ride." Her lips parted in a huge grin. "Or should I cancel?" She winked, unabashed at catching them in a very naked position. "Did you like using the crop?" The pregnant bar owner glanced around. "What? No chaps? Next time you'll have to wear those, Jessie." Audrey rubbed her hand over her stomach. "So, do you need a ride or not?"

Jessie's legs tightened around Brody and she pressed her chest to his, to hide as much of her bare body from view. "Yes, I'll need that ride."

"No she won't," Brody insisted. "I'll see her home." He glanced at Audrey. "If you'll leave us, we'll dress and get out of your storeroom."

"No need to hurry." She glanced around the packed

room. "There's something about this room that inspires orgasms."

Jessie glanced over Brody's shoulder and caught Audrey's gaze. "I'll need that ride."

Brody scowled. "We'll talk about it."

"Well, I'll wait outside, unless you want me to watch? Some couples get off better with an audience." Audrey's eyes were wide, hopeful. "I know Jackson and I do."

"We prefer privacy," Brody assured her.

Audrey laughed. "Should have thought of that before you got it on in my storeroom." She held up her hand. "No worries. I'll leave you two to it." She backed out of the room, her gaze on them until the door closed.

"That was awkward." Jessie leaned back, her cheeks burning.

Brody slipped out of her, his cock still stiff and glistening with their juices. He stepped back and zipped his jeans, and then reached for Jessie, helping her off the stack of boxes and onto her feet. "You'd better get dressed." He held on to her long enough for her to get her balance on shaking legs.

She'd been thoroughly fucked and her pussy throbbed in gratitude. But life went on and she needed to do some thinking.

Alone.

Jessie tugged the dress over her head and glanced around for her panties. When she couldn't find them, she gave up. She was headed back to the ranch to pack. Going commando for a short time wouldn't kill her. Staying with Brody, when he'd be leaving soon, would take a slice right out of her heart. She'd be better off leaving before he did.

Working at the ranch after he left, where everything reminded her of him, would kill her. If his family knew how much Brody meant to her, it was highly likely they'd pity her. Pity was the last thing she wanted from the McFarlans.

"I have to go."

"I'm taking you home."

"No, you need to stay and make sure Colin gets home okay. He's been drinking too much to drive," she lied.

"I'll get Angus to come pick him up." His face hardened. "I'm taking you home."

Her heart thrilled a little at Brody's determination. Yet, she had to remind herself he'd made no declarations of love like "let's try for happily ever after" or even "I'll see you tomorrow".

When she turned to leave, he gripped her arm. "What just happened..." Brody paused and then continued, "...I didn't come in here intending to make love to you—only to talk."

"I can't," she said, her eyes blurring. "I can't do this."

"Do what? If you don't want me to make love to you, I won't. But please. Come home."

"It's not my home, Brody. And I can't be there as long as you are."

He reached out to take her into his arms, but she sidestepped around him and ran for the door.

Before she could open it, he pressed his hand to the wooden panel. "I don't understand."

"You don't have to. You're going back to Seattle and I need to move on." Jessie swallowed hard to keep the sob from rising up her throat. "Now, if you'll excuse me."

"I'm taking you home, Jessie. And we're going to talk about this."

She tried to open the door, but it wouldn't budge with him leaning on it. "Okay." She ducked her head and lied, "I need to visit the restroom and collect my purse behind the bar."

For a moment, he continued leaning on the door. Finally, he straightened and opened the door for her. "I'll be waiting."

Jessie scurried through the door and down the hallway, hurried over to the ladies' room and was practically knocked over by Audrey coming out.

Audrey smiled. "Sorry. That must have been my tenth trip tonight." Her grin faded when she took in Jessie's face.

She hooked Jessie's arm and turned right around and reentered the bathroom. "What's wrong?"

"Oh, Audrey!" Jessie burst into tears and ran into a stall, slamming the door behind her.

"Now, how am I supposed to help you if I don't know what's wrong?" Audrey said, her feet appearing below the stall door. "Come out and talk to me."

Jessie couldn't stop sobbing long enough to say anything. Every time she opened her mouth, another sob emerged.

"Jessie, honey, I can't stand to see anyone cry. It upsets me." Audrey knocked softly. "And if I'm upset, the baby's upset. Please, for the sake of Jackson Jr., open the door and let's work this out."

Guilt trumped sorrow and Jessie opened the stall door.

Audrey held open her arms and Jessie fell into them, careful not to bump the baby.

"Ah, sweetie, nothing can be that bad."

"It is."

"Tell me about it."

"I…I…" Jessie hiccupped, "…I think I'm in love." And tears flowed all over again.

Audrey chuckled softly, rubbing her hand over Jessie's hair. "Baby, is that all? You should be happy. Not everyone finds someone who makes them crying-buckets-of-tears-in-love." She tipped Jessie's chin. "I hope it's Brody McFarlan."

Jessie nodded.

"Then why are you crying?"

"He doesn't love me."

Audrey's eyes widened. "What do you mean? From what I saw, he was loving the stuffin' out of you in the storeroom." She winked.

"He never said so…and…and…he's leaving for Seattle as soon as he can." Jessie straightened and scrubbed her hands over her face. "I can't stay at the Rafter M. Do you know anywhere I can stay until I figure out where to go next? I only have a little money I made from working."

"Honey, you can stay with me and Jackson for the time being. Mark's waiting to take you home now."

"Brody thinks he's taking me."

"I'll sneak you out the back and have Mark pick you up there."

"Are you sure I should stay with you? You don't need my drama in your life. You're about to have all you can handle. I need to find a place that can take Scout, my horse."

Audrey hugged her again. "I could use a little help around the house. I'm finding it harder to keep up, and Jackson has turned all my white things pink when he lends a hand with the laundry. And we have just the place for Scout. I'll have Mark and Luke go get him tomorrow."

"It's too much." Jessie shook her head. "I can't impose."

"I insist and Jackson will too." She turned Jessie toward the door. "Now, come on. I have to get you out of here without you being seen. Hide behind me. I'm as big as a barn. No one will notice you."

"Don't be silly. The only big part of you is your baby bump."

"You're a doll. I'm going to keep you around for an ego boost." Audrey peeked out the door. "Brody's talking to his brothers. Make a run for it and I'll round up Mark."

Keeping her head low, Jessie ran for the hallway leading to the back exit. She didn't stop until she stood on the back porch and stared out at the big Texas sky full of stars, her heart heavy. In the short time she'd been with the McFarlans, she'd felt more at home than anywhere else she'd lived. She should have known better than to fall in love with a cowboy and his family.

Mrs. McFarlan had been like the mother she never knew.

Tears welled in her eyes and slipped down her cheeks. Yeah, her daddy would have been appalled, but she just couldn't stop them from falling.

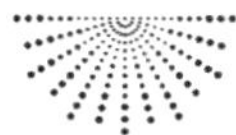

CHAPTER ELEVEN

Brody left the storeroom and returned to the bar, his body still pulsing to the rhythm of their lovemaking. He thought that they'd been good together, that he'd given her as much pleasure as she'd given him.

Then why the hell had she been so determined to leave? "Damn."

He glanced around the saloon, searching for Angus. He hadn't seen his older brother since they entered the building together. Maybe he could make sense of women. Brody sure as hell couldn't.

Colin stood by a table in the far corner talking to Connor Mason and Ed Judson. He smiled and laughed, all the while his gaze kept slipping to the bar where Fancy Wilson sat nursing a longneck.

Brody still cared for Fancy, but not like a fiancée. More like a good friend. He should have seen back when they were dating that they were more friends than lovers and a marriage between them wouldn't last. They both deserved to find deep and lasting love with someone who rocked their worlds.

"You look like someone just ran over your favorite dog." Angus's hand descended on Brody's shoulder. "Let me buy you a beer."

"I don't need one. I'm leaving soon." He glanced toward the hallway where the bathrooms were located. He'd seen Jessie headed that way. As soon as she came out, he'd take her back to the ranch and get things out in the open. Not that he had a clue what those things were.

"Jessie leave?" Angus asked.

"Not yet."

"I'm missing Gwen tonight. I'll be glad when we're married and living under the same roof." Angus sat on a barstool and ordered a beer, then turned to Brody. "So, what's going on between you and Jessie?"

Brody ran a hand through his hair and stared at the hallway to the bathrooms, wondering how long it took to use the facilities. "I don't know."

"I could swear there was some chemistry going on when you were dancing with her."

"I thought so too." And then they'd made love and the woman had run like a skittish doe.

"Do you think there's a chance you might be falling for her?" Angus tipped his bottle, appearing casual, like Brody's answer didn't mean a thing.

Brody knew better. He faced Angus. "Mom's threat aside, I don't know what I'm feeling for Jessie. All I know is she's got me all knotted up inside."

Libby, the bartender, popped the top off a longneck and set it in front of him.

Angus raised his own bottle toward Brody. "Here's to finding the girl you love."

Frowning down at the bottle, Brody said, "I don't want to get involved, because I don't plan on staying any longer than necessary."

"Do you really have to go back to Seattle?"

"It's where I belong."

"Are you sure?" Angus asked. "Do you have a house, some friends and a woman waiting for you?"

Brody lived in a sparsely furnished apartment. His art supplies and his clothes were the most personal things he owned. He had a few friends. Okay, so he had one. The art dealer who'd seen something in his work and encouraged him to display it in the galleries in Seattle, Vancouver, San Francisco and all along the West Coast. But she was fifty something and happily single. So, did he have someone waiting for him in Seattle?

"No, I don't own a house or have anyone waiting for me in Seattle."

"Then why don't you stay?" Angus stared at him for a moment. "Or are you still feuding with Colin?"

Brody glanced toward Colin. All the anger he still harbored when he returned to the Rafter M had disappeared. Granted, his relationship with Colin would never be as close as it had been when they were kids, but he didn't hate him.

If he was honest with himself, Brody was happy to see both of his brothers, and being around them reminded him he still had family and they would always be there for him.

"No. I'm not feuding with Colin."

"You might want to let Colin know. For the past eight years, he's been beating himself up for whatever happened between the two of you."

"I was a fool," Brody said. "Fancy was never right for me. We were better friends than we would have been husband and wife."

"I think she was on the verge of telling you when she ran into Colin that night."

Brody nodded. "I knew it wasn't right. But I was young and stupid, and I didn't want to admit I was wrong. I waited too long."

And now he was waiting too long to make things right with Jessie. But what was he feeling? Was it love or just lust? He faced Angus. "How do you know you're in love?"

Angus shrugged. "That's easy. When every minute you're away from her, you think about her."

The entire week he avoided Jessie, she'd been in every one of his thoughts. "And how else?" he prompted.

Angus stared at the wall in front of him. "When you make love, you can't imagine making love with anyone else. Ever again."

Making love to Jessie in the swimming hole and the storeroom had changed him forever. She responded to his touch with such passion and his body came alive in her.

"Holy shit."

"What?"

"I think I'm falling for Jessie." He shook his head. "How can it be? I've only known her for a couple weeks."

"Some say you know as soon as you meet the one."

Brody snorted, but didn't refute his brother's words. Hadn't he known Jessie was different from the first time he saw her flipping burgers, a fine sheen of perspiration glowing on her face as she smiled and served him?

"All I know is that talking about making love has gotten me so hard I can't stand it." Angus set his half-finished beer on the bar. "I have to see Gwen. Do you mind taking care of the animals in the morning?"

"No problem. Why?"

"I think I need to make a trip to Dallas tonight."

"It's pretty late," Brody noted.

Audrey walked by with Mark Gray Wolf, her head leaning toward him, her gaze intense as she spoke to her tall Kiowa brother-in-law.

"Audrey." Brody stepped in front of her.

She turned to Mark and nodded. "I'll see you later."

"Brody." Mark held out his hand. "Good to see you."

"Mark." Brody shook hands with the man, but his focus was on Audrey.

"I'd stay and buy you a beer, but Audrey's got me running errands. Later, man." Mark disappeared down the hallway leading toward the storeroom.

Audrey faced Brody. "What can I help you with?"

"Could you check in the ladies' bathroom for Jessie? She's been in there a long time."

Audrey's head tilted. "I'm sorry, but Jessie left."

"What?" Brody stepped back. "When? Where?"

"She went out the back door two or three minutes ago."

Brody spun and ran toward the back of the building.

Greta Sue appeared at the entrance to the hallway leading to the rear exit. "Sorry, employees only."

"Greta Sue, you have to let me through. I have to catch Jessie before it's too late."

The big woman crossed her arms. "Do you work here?"

"No."

"Then you're not going back there."

Brody could see he wasn't getting anywhere with the bouncer. He spun and weaved his way through the tables to the front exit and burst out into the parking lot.

A truck turned onto the highway, its taillights glowing a bright red as it sped away.

"Jessie!" Brody ran to catch up. By the time he reached the highway, the truck was already a quarter of a mile down the road.

His chest squeezing so tightly he couldn't breathe, Brody returned to the saloon where Colin and Angus stood by the bar.

"Where's Jessie?" Colin asked.

His chest hollow, he answered, "She's gone."

Colin's brows angled downward. "What do you mean gone? Did she find another ride home?"

He pressed a hand to his sore chest. "She's not coming home."

"Damn, Brody. Did you scare off our cook?" Colin demanded.

He nodded, his heart sore, his head reeling. "I did. But I want her back."

"If you're going to be a jerk, don't go after her," Colin said. "She's a nice kid."

"I know."

"You don't deserve her," Colin continued.

"I know," Brody repeated, dazed.

"She needs someone who'll stick around," Angus said. "She doesn't have anyone."

"And all she wanted was a place to call home," Brody whispered.

"So don't go after her if you're headed back to Seattle anyway," Angus said.

"I'm not going back to Seattle." Brody turned and walked toward the exit. "I can't let her go."

Colin caught up with him and grabbed his arm. "I won't let you hurt her anymore."

"What do you mean, anymore?"

"Whatever you did to her has her upset. Jessie's too nice for her own good. Someone needs to take care of her and keep people from hurting her."

"And you think I want to hurt her?"

"Well, from the look on her face most of the night, you already did."

"Damn." Brody stared at his brother. "Look, Colin, I'm sorry for being an ass for eight years."

"I don't give a shit about me. Don't fuck up Jessie's life."

Brody frowned. "Do you love her?"

"Don't be an ass."

Brody stiffened.

"She's a nice person and she's been through a lot." Colin touched his arm. "Jessie is like the kid sister I never had. And I protect family. So if you plan on hurting her, get ready for an ass whoopin'."

Brody grinned. "And I'll deserve one if I screw this up." He hugged his brother. "I'm going to make this right." He turned to Angus. "I'll need your help."

"I got your back, brother." Angus clapped a hand to that back. "What have you got in mind?"

"Something special. I need to find out where she went and keep her there until I get my plans in place."

Audrey Anderson Gray Wolf leaned over Brody's shoulder and said, "She's staying at my place. I'll keep her there." She patted her big belly. "Jessie can't leave if she thinks she's needed. And, boy, do I need her."

Brody hugged Audrey. "Thanks."

Audrey grinned. "And don't worry. Jackson and I will keep an eye on her."

"Good. I have work to do. My plan will take a week."

"Don't take too long. You don't want her to up and leave again," Audrey reminded him.

"I won't. I have too much riding on this." Brody hugged Angus and Colin. "I have to go. I have a lot of work to do before I see Jessie again."

THE FIRST DAY on the Gray Wolf Ranch, Jessie cleaned Audrey's house from top to bottom, cooked one of Mrs.

McFarlan's best recipes and helped Audrey get into her boots.

Luke and Mark took a horse trailer to the Rafter M Ranch and collected Scout, who was now munching happily in one of the Gray Wolf pastures.

Soon Jessie had the house in tip-top shape and drove Audrey to the saloon and back each day to keep her from getting behind. She helped out in the barn, keeping close to the house in case Audrey needed her. Jessie owed Audrey so much for taking her in when she didn't have a place to go.

A WEEK PASSED and Brody didn't call or stop by. Not that Jessie had expected him. He probably gave up on her after she ran out on him. And hadn't he said he was going back to Seattle as soon as possible?

When Jessie entered the Ugly Stick Saloon, she looked for him, hoping to catch a glimpse of the tall, handsome cowboy. She'd seen Colin and Angus, but stayed away, afraid if she talked to them, she'd start crying all over again.

On an errand in Temptation, Jessie spotted Brody's pickup at the diner. On her way back from the grocery store in Audrey's SUV, she'd pulled into the hardware store's parking space and waited, hoping Brody would emerge before she had to leave.

When he did, Jessie's heart sank to her knees.

Brody held the door open for a smiling, laughing woman. Fancy Wilson.

Jessie pulled out of the parking space and sped back

to the Gray Wolfs' ranch and did her best to avoid Temptation for the rest of the week.

AUDREY CAME to her Saturday morning with a request. "A friend of mine has some artwork in a gallery in Dallas. Do you mind driving me there and back?"

Jessie frowned. "I'm not much good driving in heavy traffic."

"It's Saturday. At the very least it won't be rush-hour traffic. Please? Jackson doesn't want me behind the wheel and I promised my friend I'd go and show my support. Jackson was going to take me, but one of the bulls broke through a fence and is raising hell on the neighbor's ranch. He's not going to make it."

"You know I don't mind. You've done so much for me." Jessie hugged the woman. "When do we leave?"

"This afternoon at four. The showing starts at six." Audrey grinned, and shivered with excitement. "I can't wait. I haven't seen his work yet, but I hear he's really very good."

Jessie forced a smile, not feeling at all excited about driving all the way to Dallas and back that evening. What she wanted to do was crawl into her bed and hide until her heart stopped hurting. But she couldn't wallow in self-pity. Life went on.

Time would help heal her heart and the sooner Brody left for Seattle, the sooner she would quit looking for him everywhere she went.

THAT AFTERNOON, Jessie stood in the bedroom, her hair hanging wet down her back, fresh from a shower, wearing shorts and an oversized blue-chambray shirt. She held up the two dresses Mrs. McFarlan insisted she buy at the thrift store, wondering what someone wore to an art gallery showing.

The first dress she hung back in the closet, her hand stroking the fabric, bringing back memories of her and Brody making love in the storeroom of the Ugly Stick.

A lump formed in her throat and Jessie had to bite down on her bottom lip to keep it from trembling.

Not one call. Nothing. It was as if Brody had already left for Seattle.

"I was thinking this would look nice on you." Audrey appeared in the doorway of the bedroom. "Lord knows I can't fit into it." She laughed and rubbed her big belly. "Whoa! Settle down there, Junior!" Audrey wore a black dress in flowing chiffon that fell down to just above her knees, with an empire waistline that draped over her baby bump. She held out a little black dress.

Jessie took the dress. "I can't wear anything you used to wear. You're much smaller than I ever dreamed of being."

"Not now, I'm not. That dress was a little big on me and should just fit your slim figure. Go on, try it on. You'll want to look your best. There are supposed to be a lot of wealthy people coming to the event."

Jessie pushed the dress back at Audrey. "I can wait in the SUV. I don't fit into that level of society."

"Nonsense. Besides, you have to go in with me or Jackson will make me stay home." She sighed. "Please?"

"Okay, but if it doesn't fit, I'm wearing the other dress."

"Trust me, you'll want to wear the little black dress for this. It's a very posh gallery." Audrey lifted a strand of Jessie's wet hair. "Before you dress, let me help you do your hair."

"What's wrong with letting it dry naturally?"

"Honey, you have beautiful hair. For this occasion, let me take a flat iron to it just to make it lay perfectly straight. A little makeup and you'll look like a million bucks."

"I don't own any makeup."

"Sweetie, I do."

Audrey led her into the master bedroom's bathroom and went to work on Jessie like she was her latest science project. When she was finished, she refused to let Jessie look in the mirror until she had her dress on.

"There is a pair of strappy, low-heel, rhinestone sandals in the bottom of my closet. I'll let you dig them out while I empty my bladder for the hundredth time today. Then we can hit the road."

Jessie found the sandals. The heart of the girlie girl she'd buried beneath her blue jeans fluttered at the bling sparkling in the light. She hurried to her bedroom and slipped into the black dress and sandals. Just like Audrey predicted, the dress fit her like a glove, molding to her body's curves.

She tugged at the fabric, preferring her jeans, loose blouses and worn cowboy boots. But this night was for Audrey, the woman who'd done so much for her. Jessie wouldn't complain.

THE DRIVE into Dallas was uneventful. Most of the traffic was headed the opposite direction as night fell over the city.

Audrey squirmed in the passenger seat, glowing with excitement. "I can't wait to get there."

Following the GPS mounted on the dash, Jessie made it into the heart of Dallas and found the building. She parked the SUV in a parking garage and helped Audrey out.

Audrey laughed, bubbling with excitement Jessie couldn't get in to. "First stop is the ladies' room."

The huge oil paintings in the windows of the gallery were of fields of blue bonnets and pastures of Bermuda hay bent in the wind. The images reminded her of the day she had ridden out across the Rafter M Ranch on Scout.

Jessie's chest felt like someone had it in an iron grip, squeezing hard. She almost backed out. She could fake a stomachache and offer to sit in the vehicle in the parking garage.

One look at Audrey's face, and Jessie knew she couldn't disappoint her friend.

"Oh my. He's wonderful! I never knew B—he had it in him. Look at the live oak tree in the field. It looks real, like I could feel the bark." Audrey hurried for the door.

Jessie followed. The crowd inside wore designer suits and cocktail dresses, making Jessie glad she'd worn Audrey's dress. Her sundress would have looked like what it was, a thrift-store hand-me-down.

"Jessie, honey!" a familiar female voice called out.

Mrs. McFarlan engulfed her in a bear hug that left her breathless. "I miss having you around the house. When are you coming home?"

"It's good to see you too, Mrs. M." Jessie returned the woman's hug, that perpetual lump in her throat refusing to budge. Her gaze panned the room, her heart pounding against her ribs as she searched the faces for Brody's.

"It's too bad Brody didn't come with us," Mrs. M licked her lips, shifted her eyes and went on. "Maybe if he'd known you were going to be here, he'd have changed his mind. Isn't this exciting? I've never been to an art gallery before. Angus and Colin brought me as a special treat."

Jessie's hopes plummeted.

"I'll be right back," Audrey assured her. "Go on in without me."

Angus and Colin stood in front of a painting of an old barn that appeared vaguely familiar. Jessie excused herself from Mrs. M and angled away from the McFarlans, heading into a different room, separate from the huge front room of the gallery. The lighting was muted, a soft, luminescent glow from the recessed bulbs in the ceiling. Each painting had special lights shining on it.

Too upset to care about what was on the canvases, it was several moments before the images caught her attention.

Jessie gasped at a painting of a brindle horse rearing into the sunshine, its dark mane and tail flying out.

She'd recognize Scout anywhere, with the caramel-colored blaze on his forehead. The artist had captured the animal's beauty as well as his spirit. The woman standing in front of the animal had long, flowing blonde hair caught by the wind. Her hand was raised to calm the horse. Jessie recognized herself and could feel the love the woman in the painting had for the horse.

For several long minutes, Jessie studied the bold strokes. Curious about the other paintings in the room now, she moved to the next and gasped.

A green canopy hovered over a blue-green pool of water. Sunshine dappled the ripples on the surface where there was a simmering image of a naked woman floating on her back, her blonde hair fanning around her. Though she was naked, her private parts were strategically concealed beneath the ripples of water and dark shading of the overhanging branches. The image invited her to step into the painting and dive into the pool. She could feel the cool water swirling around like it had that day she'd been skinny-dipping in the swimming hole. The painting was of her, the woman's eyes were closed, but Jessie knew—the painting was her.

The next painting was a close-up of her face, gray-blue eyes staring back at her as if from a mirror. Only the painting showed *more*. Jessie could see past the eyes into the soul of the woman on the canvas, and her heart ached with the beauty of each stroke of the artist's brush.

Moving to the next painting, she saw herself with her head thrown back, her eyes alight, the gray irises nearly black with passion.

Her pulse pounding, core tightening, she relived the

intensity of making love to Brody amongst the stacks of boxes in the saloon storeroom. Her breath caught and held, and she pressed a hand to her chest in a half-assed attempt to still her thundering heart.

Footsteps sounded, headed her way. Even before she turned, Jessie knew who stood behind her as electricity filled the air. She turned and her heart broke all over again. Brody stood there in a black tuxedo, his dark hair slicked back and his brown eyes dark pools of secrets. God, he was so beautiful it made her want to cry all over again.

BRODY HAD BEEN WATCHING for Jessie. When she arrived, he'd stood back, out of her view, observing her reaction to the paintings. As she passed each canvas, he felt as if he'd exposed another part of him, peeling back the layers of the walls he'd constructed around himself and the art he'd learned was so much a part of him.

He'd spent the past week and a half painting, amassing a collection of images that haunted him during the day and well after he fell asleep at night.

The room Jessie now stood in was his best work, every stroke coming straight from his heart.

When she turned to face him, he held his breath, afraid she'd be offended at how he'd depicted her in oil. He felt he'd made himself vulnerable to her, exposing his heart for the world to see. He'd painted these creations as a way to express how deep his emotions ran for Jessie.

Would she see what he did and know what it meant to him?

Her gaze rose to meet his, her face full of wonder. "You painted all of these?"

He nodded.

She turned to the painting of her face glowing with passion, her lips parted in a soft O as she succumbed to desire. "They're so real…and…beautiful." Jessie reached toward the painting as if to touch the woman.

Brody took her outstretched hand. "You're not mad I painted you without your permission?"

"Mad?" She snorted and stared up at him, shaking her head. "I'm stunned. But you have it all wrong. I'm not nearly that beautiful." She touched her hand to her straightened hair, heat rising into her cheeks.

He tugged her toward him and lifted her chin with his finger. "If you could see what I see, you'd know the paintings speak the truth."

"You see me like that?" she whispered, her gaze shifting to his lips. Hunger burning from her gray-blue eyes.

Brody brushed his mouth across hers, tempted to forget everything else, but he couldn't. Not until he said what he'd rehearsed a thousand times that day. He had to get it right, or risk losing the woman who'd fed his muse, breathed passion into his work and made him want to be a better man.

"Jessie, ever since I met you, my thoughts have been all over the place. I didn't want to come home, and once I did, I didn't want to stay."

She drew in a sharp breath and nodded, her bottom lip trembling so slightly he thought he'd imagined it…

until she bit down on it. "You always said you weren't staying."

Lifting her hands to his lips, he stepped closer. "Then I met a sassy cowgirl who could grill a burger like nobody's business but couldn't cook in a kitchen to save her life."

Her brows knit and she stared down at where his hands held hers. "I'm learning," she said, her voice catching.

"I don't care if you burn every meal. You taught me something more important than putting dinner on the table." He tipped her chin up, forcing her to stare into his eyes. "You taught me how lucky I am to have a family, and not to neglect those very important relationships. They might not be around forever."

Her lips quirked on the edges. "That was a no-brainer."

"Maybe to you, but I was too busy thinking of myself to look around and care about others." He cupped her cheek in his hand. "You also reminded me that home truly is where the heart is."

"Would that be in Seattle?" she asked so softly he barely heard her words.

Brody shook his head. "No."

She glanced around the room. "Dallas?"

"No." He brushed his lips across hers. "It's anywhere you are."

"Me?" she said, touching a hand to her breast. Tears welled in her eyes. "But you're going back to Seattle."

"If I asked you to go with me, would you?"

She stared at him for a long time. "Don't tease me,

Brody. I couldn't bear it if you were only pulling my leg."

"You didn't answer me," he prompted.

"Would Scout be welcome? He's all the family I have left."

"Scout will always be welcome."

"Then, yes." She slid her hands around his neck. "Yes, Scout and I would follow you to Seattle, Bozeman, San Francisco and Timbuktu." She leaned her forehead against the lapels of his suit. "Just don't leave without me because, you see, I've made the ultimate blunder and fallen in love with you, your mother and your two brothers. I want to be with you and all of your family."

He drew her into his arms and cradled the back of her head. "It's a good thing, darlin', because I plan on staying at the Rafter M Ranch for a very long time and I want you with me."

A sob rising up her throat, Jessie flung herself into his arms and clung to him.

He kissed her long and hard, his tongue pushing past her teeth to claim hers.

Brody forgot where he was and would have gone on all night, kissing Jessie, but someone cleared her throat at the other end of the room, breaking through the haze of happiness.

His mother stood in the entrance to the room, Colin and Angus at her side. She beamed from ear to ear, touching a hand to her chest. "Oh, Brody. I didn't know you had so much talent. I'm your mother. I should know these things."

Brody pulled Jessie into the crook of his arm and

faced his family. "I didn't tell anyone. The only reason Angus knew was because he caught me red-handed with my paints, canvas and easel out at the hunting cabin."

"Why didn't you tell us you were so well-known?"

He shrugged. "I wasn't sure how you and my brothers would react to finding out your son and their brother was an artist."

"Are you kidding me?" Colin burst into the room and hugged Brody, pounding him on the back. "I can't get over what you've accomplished. It's…" he shook his head, "…it's amazing. And to think, I knew Brody McFarlan when he was a country boy on the ranch." He grinned and glanced at the paintings in the room, his eyes rounding. "Wow. And these are even better than the landscapes."

Angus, Colin and Mrs. M studied the paintings, their brows furrowing.

Mrs. M was first to say something as she stood in front of the creek painting. "Is this who I think it is?" She faced Jessie and winked. "You're beautiful, my dear. And it might interest you to know that Brody was conceived in that pool."

Angus and Colin both studied the painting and looked back at Jessie.

"I don't know if I'd want my girlfriend's naked body hanging in an art gallery for all to see," Colin said.

"You can't see anything important," Jessie said. "And I'm flattered he made me look better than I really look."

Angus and Colin both stared at her.

"You're kidding, right?" Angus said.

"Have you looked in the mirror lately?" Colin asked. "You're freakin' gorgeous."

Jessie's cheeks reddened. "Thank you."

"If you'll excuse us, I wanted to show Jessie something." Brody grabbed Jessie's hand and led her toward the door.

BEHIND THEM, Mrs. M said, "Two down. One to go."

Jessie glanced over her shoulder, wondering what the woman meant.

Mrs. McFarlan had leveled her gaze on Colin. "You'd better get busy. The two months are almost up."

Curious, Jessie almost stopped to ask, but Brody had other plans for her and she didn't want to let him out of her sight.

He led her through the gallery, waylaid by half a dozen people who wanted to congratulate him on his work and increasing sales.

Brody nodded politely, thanked them and pressed forward.

At the back of the gallery was a hall with a door at the end. He didn't slow until they were through the door. He closed and locked it behind them.

"What is it you wanted to show me?" Jessie asked, glancing around a darkened room with a long white-leather couch and mahogany desk. "Did you save one of your paintings in here?"

"No. I wanted to do this." Brody pulled her into his arms and kissed her all over again.

She gripped the lapels of his tuxedo and dragged him down, kissing him back. When she came up to catch a breath, she asked, "The door's locked?"

He nodded, breathing fast, his cock pressing against the zipper of his trousers.

Jessie shoved the jacket over his shoulders and hung it on a coatrack in the corner. Then she reached behind her, fumbling for the zipper on the back of her dress.

"Here." Brody's hands descended on her arms and he turned her. "Let me."

In one long, slow glide, he lowered the zipper all the way down her back to the top of the rounded swells of her ass, the crease clearly visible.

Brody's groin tightened and his cock grew rock-hard.

She wasn't wearing panties beneath the slim-fitting black dress.

He groaned and slipped a hand inside the zipper, cupping her bottom. "Sweet Jessie."

Brody brushed aside her hair and nuzzled the back of her neck.

She shrugged out of the dress and let the front fall, catching on her hips.

Not only was she pantyless, she wasn't wearing a bra. She raised his hands to cup her breasts and leaned into him, her head falling back onto his shoulder. "Shouldn't you be out there with your fans?" she said, her words more a sexy moan, her hand guiding his down to the juncture of her thighs.

"I'm right where I'm supposed to be," he said, sliding a finger between her folds, stroking the sliver of flesh that made her chest expand with an indrawn breath.

"You aren't going back to Seattle?"

"No," he whispered into her ear. "Everything I need is here."

He pushed her dress over her hips and it slid to the floor around her ankles. Brody swung her up into his arms, strode across the floor to the huge mahogany desk and sat her on the edge of the smooth surface.

She parted her knees, her sexy sandals sparkling in the muted light from a corner lamp. Jessie reached for the buttons on his shirt and flicked them open one at a time. "I missed you."

"Will you be satisfied with an artist for the man in your life?"

"You'll always be the cowboy I fell for, and more. These hands..." she held one up and drew her finger along the lifeline in his palm and out to the tips of his fingers, "...are even more remarkable than I'd given them credit for. And they were pretty amazing to begin with."

"I'm learning that with the right muse, there's no end to what I can do." He cupped her cheek and bent to capture her lips.

She reached for the button on his trousers and pushed it through the hole, then slid his zipper down. His cock sprang free and she wrapped her hand around its hard length, guiding him home.

As he thrust into her, he knew this was where he

belonged. With her. In Texas. Surrounded by the family he loved.

**If you enjoyed this book, try the other books in the
Ugly Stick Saloon Series**

Boots & Chaps (#1)
Boots & Sex Ed (#2)
Boots & Leather (#3)
Boots & Promises (#4)
Boots & Bareback (#5)
Boots & Dirty Tricks (#6)
Boots & Lace (#7)
Boots & Roses (#8)
Boots & Buckles (#9)
Boots & the Wishes (#10)
Boots & Twisters (#11)
Boots & the Bachelor (#12)
Boots & The Rogue (#13)
Boots & The Heartbreaker (#14)
Boots & Wings (#15)

BOOTS & THE HEARTBREAKER

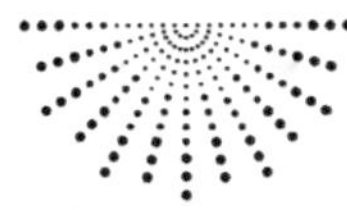

UGLY STICK SALOON SERIES BOOK #14

by Elle James
New York Times Bestselling Author

writing as

Myla Jackson

BOOTS
& the
HEARTBREAKER
UGLY STICK SALOON
New York Times Bestselling Author
ELLE JAMES
writing as
MYLA JACKSON

CHAPTER ONE

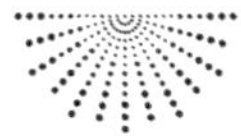

Colin McFarlan stared into his beer. The pressure was on.

"It's your turn." His brother Angus nudged him in the side. "I've got Gwen and Dalton. Brody has Jessie. There's only three weeks left in Mom's ultimatum."

"Tell me about it." He lifted his long neck bottle and swiveled on the bar stool at the Ugly Stick Saloon.

The usual Friday night crowd did nothing to boost his spirits. Sure, there were ladies in the bar, but half of them were already taken.

"What about the Banks twins?" Brody nodded toward the gorgeous blond-haired, blue-eyed identical twins giggling at something Sam Whitefeather was telling them.

"I don't know." Colin cringed. "They're so young."

"Young?" Angus snorted. "Since when does that bother you? Besides they're both twenty-two and legal, freshly home from college."

Colin took a long swig of his beer and rolled it around in his mouth before swallowing. "I'm just not feeling it."

"What's to feel?" Angus asked. "You find a woman, get engaged and be done with it. Mom will be happy, she'll stop making insane threats of selling off the ranch, and we can all get back to work without worrying about having our home sold out from under us."

"Yeah, what's keeping you?" Brody, the middle brother sat on the other side of Colin. "You've always loved women."

"Right. Women. Plural of woman." Colin pushed a hand through his hair. He'd always played the field, dating a woman for no more than three dates before cutting her loose. He'd always found something not quite right about the fit, and didn't want any clingy goodbyes.

No single woman had captured his attention and kept it. Except one. Fancy Wilson.

No sooner had he thought of her, the woman on his mind walked through the entrance, smiling up at Dusty Cramer, the local sheriff's deputy on a rare Friday night off duty.

Damn. There went Colin's evening. He had just about talked himself into asking one of the Banks twins to dance. Now, all desire to dance with Hayley or Alexis fled. How could he dance with them when all he could think about was how beautiful Fancy looked in a tight, blue jean skirt and cowboy boots?

The real estate agent, who usually wore a pencil skirt and suit jacket, and made them look sexy as hell, appeared even more amazing in the casual attire. She reminded him of that one night eight years ago that had changed his life.

The night she'd called off her engagement to his brother Brody.

The same night she'd cried in Colin's arms and they'd made love.

He'd gone from happy-go-lucky to destroying his brother's trust and losing the girl he'd fallen for. Brody moved to the west end of the country and refused to come home.

It had taken eight years and his mother's ultimatum to bring Brody back.

Fancy had left town not long after Brody, moving to Dallas to start over.

Colin knew that because he'd heard through his mother's grapevine. Not only had she started over, she'd done pretty well for herself selling real estate. Why she'd decided to return to Temptation was beyond Colin's comprehension. She could make so much more money in Dallas, and marry the high-powered man of her dreams. A small town girl making it in the big D.

A fuckin' Cinderella story.

Colin's gaze captured Fancy's for a moment. Then she turned to Dusty and laughed up at him, her smile wide, green eyes twinkling. Since she'd been back in Temptation, she'd dyed her hair back from auburn to her natural blond. The woman would look good in black, brown, auburn or blond hair. Hell, she'd probably look good bald and with half her teeth, just to make Colin more miserable.

"What's wrong, Colin?" Angus leaned close. "You look like you ate a lemon. Are the Banks girls really all that bad?"

Colin straightened and set the beer bottle on the bar. "Not at all. I think I'll ask them to dance."

"Both of them?" Brody laughed. "Might be a little hard to do in a two-step."

"Not a problem. They're playing 'Cotton-eyed Joe.'" Colin pushed to his feet and strode across the floor, refusing to glance Fancy's way, although he could see her in his peripheral vision.

He stopped in front of Hayley. Or was it Alexis? It didn't matter. "Would you two care to dance?"

The two young women squealed delightedly and jumped to their feet. "Of course we would," they said in unison.

Oh good, he'd get matching comments in stereo. Colin's jaw tightened to keep from saying anything disparaging to the women. He just wasn't in the mood for any of this.

He led them onto the dance floor, spun them both out and back into the curve of his arms. They giggled and settled into the dance, kicking their heels, backing up then moving forward, shouting "bullshit!" when it came to that part in the song.

An accomplished dancer, Colin could do the moves with his eyes closed and was tempted to do just that to avoid making eye contact with Fancy.

If having his old flame in the saloon wasn't hard enough on Colin's nerves, Fancy and Dusty stepped onto the dance floor as the song transitioned into a waltz.

"I'll just sit this one out," Alexis said.

"Thanks, dear." Hayley molded her body against Colin's and pressed her cheek to his chest. "Umm. You feel amazing."

Colin muttered something, not even aware of the woman in his arms, his entire attention on how low Dusty's hand was on the small of Fancy's back.

Anger simmered below the surface and Colin's muscles tensed. If Dusty's hand drifted any lower...

"Colin, sweetie, I didn't know you and the boys would be here tonight." Maggie McFarlan, Colin's mother, danced by in Carl Landers's arms. Dressed in a flirty white dress that came down to her knees and some brand-spanking-new red cowboy boots, she looked half her age.

What the hell?

Colin danced Hayley—or was it Alexis—around faster to catch up to the older couple whirling around the dance floor.

He caught up when Carl swung his mother way out and back in, dipping her low in his arms.

"Mom? What are you doing here?" Colin demanded.

His mother smiled up at him, deep in the dip, Carl holding her effortlessly. "Why, I think it would be obvious. I'm dancing!" She laughed as Carl drew her up in his arms and whirled her around again.

Colin whipped Hayley-Alexis around and practically ran to keep up with Carl. "I thought we talked about this."

"You talked. I ignored." She glared at him. "Now stop interrupting this lovely dance."

Stopping in the middle of the floor, with Hayley-Alexis frowning in his arms, his mother dancing with Temptation's infamous heartbreaker and Fancy so close to Dusty they might as well be having sex on the dance floor, Colin didn't know whether to throw his hands in the air, or throw a punch.

"If you don't want to dance, just say so." Hayley-Alexis smiled up at him. "We can sit this one out. Maybe have a drink and just talk."

"What?" He stared down at the woman he'd asked to dance. "I'm sorry. I need to sit this one out." Colin walked her back to the table where her sister bounced to her feet.

"Is it my turn?" the other twin asked.

Colin didn't stop to answer, weaving his way through the tables to the bar.

"What can I get for you?" Libby the bartender asked.

"Give me a whiskey," he said and took the stool beside Angus. "Hell, make it a double."

Angus sat with his back to the bar. "I don't know what she sees in him."

With his focus on Libby and the whiskey she poured into a tumbler, Colin responded. "He's not right for her."

"Got that right." Brody tipped is beer and drank a swallow before pointing the mug at the dance floor. "He's too suave. You know. He's got city slicker written all over him."

"I wouldn't call him suave." Colin grabbed the

whiskey from Libby's hand and tossed back half the glass before swiveling to face the dancers. "And he's no city slicker."

"You don't think so?" Angus shook his head. "He's holding her so close you'd have to use a pry bar to break them up. Doesn't it make you want to punch his lights out?"

Colin threw back the rest of the whiskey and pushed to his feet. "Damn right it does."

Brody reached out and grabbed Colin's arm. "You're not going to hit him, are you?"

"No. Hitting an officer of the law isn't something I'm willing to spend time in jail for."

Angus's brows twisted. "Since when is Landers an officer of the law?"

Colin stared at his older brother like he'd stepped out of another world. "What are you talking about?"

"Landers and Mom." Augus laughed.

"Landers and Mom?" Colin shifted his gaze to the older couple in a clench that would embarrass his grandmother. "Holy hell. Has he no morals? That's our mother he's holding like…like… Well, hell!"

"That's who I was talking about." Angus stared at Colin. "Who has your chaps in a twist?"

"No one." Colin didn't want to admit the woman who'd come between him and Brody, was still heavy on his mind. "I'm going to dance."

"Not like that, you aren't." Angus grinned.

"What do you mean?"

"You look mad enough to spit nails. You'll scare the women away with that face."

"Thanks. But I don't need advice on how to charm women."

Angus held up his hands in surrender. "Just sayin'. You might want to tone down the madder-than-a-wet-hen look."

Colin strode through the crowded barroom, angling for the Banks twins. He'd be damned if he'd let Fancy ruin his evening of wife hunting. Three weeks. Three damn weeks before his mother followed through on her threat to sell the ranch if he and his brothers didn't have fiancées and the promise of weddings and children.

The twins were laughing at something Sam White-feather was saying again.

Colin didn't care. There were two Banks sisters. Sam could have one, Colin could take the other. Which one he got really didn't matter. They were interchangeable in Colin's mind.

He held out his hand to the one farthest from Sam. "Alexis, you wanna dance?"

The twin glanced up at him and frowned. "I'm Hayley. And no."

The other twin smiled up at him. "I'm Alexis, and if Sam isn't going to ask me to dance, I'd love to dance with you."

Hayley leaned over to her sister and muttered, "You won't be saying that for long."

Alexis shot her sister a quick frown and smiled at Sam. "Well?"

"I'll sit this one out," he said. "I'm better at riding horses than dancing."

"I'm a good teacher," Alexis offered.

"Nah." He nodded toward Colin. "Dance with McFarlan. He's the ladies' man."

Colin's gaze strayed to the dance floor where Fancy leaned against Dusty, her cheek resting on his chest.

"I guess that leaves you." Alexis extended a hand. When Colin didn't take it, she pulled it back. "Already on the dance floor before you get there, cowboy?"

Hayley mumbled, "I told you."

Not to be deterred, Alexis grabbed Colin's hand. "Come on. At least I'll get to dance, even if your mind is on another woman."

"Don't know what you're talking about," Colin grumbled.

"I'm not blind." Alexis smiled through gritted teeth. "You've been watching the blonde with Dusty since you were dancing with my sister."

Colin's gaze slipped from Fancy to Alexis and back.

Damn. She was right. He had to get a grip. Fancy had been off limits since they'd made love eight years ago. She'd gone so far as to leave Temptation, dye her hair and start a new life in Dallas. Why the hell had she come back? And worse, why had she gone back to being the blonde she was eight years ago?

"THANK you for dancing with me, Dusty," Fancy said. "I know this was supposed to be a business meeting. And I really do have a lot of properties I want to show you, but seeing Colin again just made me crazy. Thank you for agreeing to run interference."

"I don't mind playing the part of your new

boyfriend." He winked. "It means I get to dance with a pretty girl. What have you got against Colin, anyway?"

"I can't be with a man who treats every relationship so callously. I want someone who's going to stick around, be stable and not chase after every skirt as soon as he gets bored."

"You want a boring man. Like me."

Fancy gave him a twisted smile. "You're a nice man, Dusty. I don't deserve you as a friend. I just want Colin to know that I'm over him. Hopefully, when he sees me with you, he'll get the message. Then I can get on with my life."

Dusty sighed. "Must be nice to have a girl go crazy over you." He shook his head. "Can't say as I've ever had that happen. Seems I'm always the guy the girls use to make their boyfriends..." he raised his hand when Fancy opened her mouth to protest the word boyfriend in conjunction with Colin, "...ex-boyfriends or potential boyfriends jealous. Not that you're doing that, since you're over Colin, but whatever the case, I always end up the decoy."

Fancy glanced at the man whose arms held her lightly as they waltzed around the dance floor. "I'm sorry. You deserve better than that."

"I tell myself the same, but I've yet to find someone for me." Dusty raised a hand again. "Don't get me wrong. I'm not a pity case. I have a woman I visit in Hole in the Wall once a month. I satisfy my needs and she occasionally has me rescue her cat from a tree. It works." He shrugged. "For now."

"You need to find a woman who can appreciate what a wonderful man you are."

"Problem is, there are plenty of eligible bachelors in the tri-county area and fewer women."

Fancy's brows pulled together. "There's always someone for everyone. But you're right. You might have to date someone outside this area. Have you thought of spending your off time in Dallas or Austin?"

He shook his head. "Working for the sheriff's department, I work every shift at some time or another. It makes it hard to get to those places on a weekend, when most people have time off."

"You are in between a rock and a hard place." Out of the corner of her eye, Fancy could see Colin headed for the dance floor, a pretty young blonde in tow. "Smile, Dusty. As my fake date, you need to look like you're having a good time." Fancy tilted back her head and forced a laugh. "Dusty, you are so funny."

Colin swung Alexis out and back, and then danced away from Dusty and Fancy and toward his mother.

"Okay, you don't have to smile now," Fancy said. "I don't think it's me he's interested in. He's aiming for his mother and Mr. Landers."

"Mr. Landers?" Dusty tuned her, so that he could see the couple in question. "I thought you said Landers was your uncle."

Fancy nodded. "He is. But he asked me not to advertise the fact. He didn't want his reputation to taint me selling real estate in Temptation."

"How could that happen?"

"My parents' generation remembers Carl Landers as

the Heartbreaker." She chuckled. "He had all the ladies in love with him at one point or another and broke their hearts when he ended the relationships."

Dusty snorted and spun her again, keeping step with the music. "Sounds like Colin McFarlan."

"Colin?" Fancy caught a glimpse of the man cutting in on his mother's dance. "I didn't know he was a heartbreaker."

"For some reason, he and his brother Brody had a falling out eight years ago. Since then, he's dated just about every woman in the tri-county area. I think his record is three dates and he walks away."

Fancy heart fluttered. "Eight years, huh?"

"Yup. Though it looks as though he and Brody are back on speaking terms." Dusty tilted his head. "No one knows what caused the rift between the brothers." He glanced down at Fancy and smiled. "Some think it was a fight over you. After seein' you two around each other, I'm thinkin' they're right. Are they?"

Her cheeks heating, Fancy was glad the lighting was dim in the saloon. She lifted one shoulder. "People will talk. I loved Brody, but not the marryin' kind of love. More like a brother."

"And Colin?"

Mandy at the diner had also mentioned Colin's reputation. Fancy hadn't believed it. But Dusty wouldn't exaggerate. Fancy's chest hurt with the thought of Colin dating all those women. Apparently their one night together hadn't meant anything to him. She'd just been a notch on his bedpost. Swallowing a lump forming in her throat, she said, "After what you just told me about him, any girl would be a fool to fall for a guy like that. I'd just as soon keep my heart intact."

"What is he doing now, dancing with his mother?" Dusty asked.

Fancy turned. Colin broke in on his mother's and Landers's dance, leaving Fancy's uncle dancing with Alexis. What was Colin up to? He and his mother appeared to be arguing as they danced.

Fancy's uncle danced Alexis across the floor toward Fancy and stopped. "Excuse me for cutting in, but as lovely as Miss Alexis is, I don't want to be accused of being a dirty old man." He twirled Alexis toward Dusty. "Would you be so kind as to dance with this beautiful young lady?" Without waiting for a response, her uncle grabbed Fancy's hand and pulled her into a promenade hold.

Fancy glanced over her shoulder at Dusty and gave him a wan smile.

He shrugged and held out his hand to Alexis, who laughed and took it.

"What's going on?" Fancy asked her uncle.

"I think the McFarlan boys have heard of my reputation and don't approve of me as a suitor for the charming and beautiful Maggie McFarlan." His brows dipped.

"They don't think you're good enough for her?" Fancy snorted. "Maybe she's not good enough for you."

"Now sweetheart, I don't want to get sideways with the boys. They're only trying to protect their mother." He danced her, with purpose, toward Colin and his mother. "But I would like my dance partner back." He tapped on Colin's shoulder. "Pardon me, but I'm cutting in."

"Sorry," Colin said without turning around.

"Colin!" his mother said sharply. She stepped back and held out her arms to Fancy's uncle. "I would prefer to dance with Carl. Why don't you dance with Fancy? She's your age. Leave us old folks to dance with each other."

Carl smiled down at her and swept her into his arms. "You're hardly old, Maggie. Why I don't believe you've changed one bit since high school."

Maggie's cheeks flushed with color. "Oh, Carl. You're such a charmer."

The two danced away, leaving Colin and Fancy blocking the dancers on the wooden floor.

Colin held out his arms. "This can't be happening."

"What?" Fancy stepped into his arms, her heart thundering at his nearness. And she thought she'd gotten over him long ago. So much for time healing all wounds or broken hearts.

"My mother going out with the Heartbreaker."

"He's not the same person he was when he was younger," Fancy argued. After all, he was her uncle and she'd never known a nicer, more considerate man. He'd stepped up to the plate when her parents had been killed in a car wreck. The man was her surrogate father.

"What do you know about him? I thought he was just a client." Colin's brows dipped low. "You aren't dating him too, are you?"

She laughed. "Not hardly. I don't get into incest."

If possible, Colin's brows dropped even lower and

he came to a stop in the middle of the dance floor. "What do you mean, incest?"

Damn. Her uncle had wanted to spare her his reputation, and she'd gone and spilled the beans. "Carl Landers is my uncle."

"Your what?"

"Well, technically, he's my half-uncle. His dad and my mom's dad are the same person. They had different mothers. It's one of those family secrets that was amazingly well-kept."

"You're kidding."

She shook her head. "Nope."

"The situation is unacceptable. We need to talk." He grabbed her hand and led her toward the bar. "Come on."

"I'm not thirsty."

"I'm not getting you a drink." He hauled her past the bar, glanced around for Greta Sue, the bouncer who was standing at the entrance of the saloon carding everyone walking in.

"Then where are you taking me?" She tugged her arm to free it of his grip. "What if I don't want to go there?"

"We can't stand by and do nothing." Colin strode down the hallway behind the bar and threw open the first door he came to. "In here."

Fancy was practically flung into a storeroom filled with cases of booze.

Colin entered and shut the door behind him.

Alone with the man she was supposed to be getting off her mind or out of her heart, Fancy's pulse hammered against her eardrums and her palms grew moist. What was he going to do? Kiss her? Declare his undying love for her? Sweep her off her feet and tell her he couldn't live another day without her?

All those thoughts flitted through her mind as her breathing became rapid and ragged. She waited for him to turn, to show her the love still evident in his eyes.

When Colin faced her, it wasn't with love shining out of his eyes, but an angry glare. "We have to break those two up."

ABOUT THE AUTHOR

Twenty years of livin' and lovin' on a South Texas ranch raising horses, cattle, goats, ostriches and emus left an indelible impression on Myla Jackson, one she likes to instill in her red-hot stories. Myla pens wildly sexy, fun adventures of all genres including historical westerns, medieval tales, romantic suspense, contemporary romance and paranormal beasties of all shapes and sexy sizes. She lives in the tree-covered hills of Northwest Arkansas with her husband of more than 20 years and her muses—the human-wanna-be canines—Chewy and Sweetpea.

To learn more about Myla Jackson and her alter ego Elle James visit:

www.mylajackson.com
mylajackson@mylajackson.com

Ugly Stick Saloon Series

Boots & Chaps (#1)

Boots & Sex Ed (#2)

Boots & Leather (#3)

Boots & Promises (#4)

Boots & Bareback (#5)

Boots & Dirty Tricks (#6)

Boots & Lace (#7)

Boots & Roses (#8)

Boots & Buckles (#9)

Boots & the Wishes (#10)

Boots & Twisters (#11)

Boots & the Bachelor (#12)

Boots & The Rogue (#13)

Boots & The Heartbreaker (#14)

Boots & Wings (#15)

Tomb Raider Trouble

Trouble with Harry

Trouble with Will

Trouble with Mitch

Bound and Tied

Honor Bound

Duty Bound

River Bound

Paranormal

Shewolf

Thorn's Kiss

Sex, Lies & Vampire Hunters

www.ingramcontent.com/pod-product-compliance
Lightning Source LLC
Chambersburg PA
CBHW070504120726
47910CB00003B/1117